The Avenger in the Rye

Cliff Roberts

DEDICATION

This book is dedicated to my wife, Karla. For all the times I didn't say thank you, thank you.

Special thanks to three women, without whom this book would still be a rough, rough draft on my laptop. Jill Snapp, Vonne Karraker, and Janna Hagerty, the value of your help is difficult for me to convey in words. So, hugs all around!

Cliff Roberts

The Avenger in the Rye

CHAPTER 1

The day it happened started like most other days, but that changed the moment his wife got home that evening. Dwight had gotten off work at 3pm, and made it to the school by 3:10. He waited to pick Abigail up in a line of parents in cars that stretched around the block. After three decades of having parents pick up their kids at 3 p.m.at this school, the latest people in charge decided it was safer and easier if they had all the parents line up in their cars at one single point to give away one kid at a time. You could get there 30 minutes early and be first in line, or 30 minutes late and be last in line. The school discouraged parking nearby and walking to pick up your child as it somehow confused the situation. Several rebel parents did it anyway, suffering glares from the teachers as well as parents waiting in the car line. Dwight had done it in the beginning, parking half a block away and walking to get Abby. He had been quite proud of himself for rescuing them from a

30 minute wait and saving time and gas. He had told Marlene about his brashness and she had thrown a fit. She said he was breaking the rules, and the teachers might take it out on Abigail. Dwight honestly didn't see how they would get their revenge for his defiance by taking it out on a 7-year-old girl, but he honestly didn't understand a lot of the things that made Marlene mad at him. Now he waited in line like the rest of them, where he and the teachers sent hot stares at the line-cutters and rule breakers who still had nerve enough to go against the public education system.

This day he waited in the line like he was supposed to, and as he got closer he looked for Abigail in the line of children waiting to be picked up. He spotted her bouncing up and down with another girl like two jumping beans, and he smiled. They seemed to be having a contest of some kind. They both were laughing and trying to push each other over. Then a boy got between them and started bouncing with them. Abigail grabbed him by his backpack and spun him around until he was out of the way. They laughed because he kept spinning on purpose, and then they went back to jumping. Dwight pulled up to the head of the line as the line supervisor/teacher waved him emphatically forward. Abigail said goodbye to her still-jumping friend and clambered into the back seat of his truck.

"Did you see me? Emma and me were playing a jumping game to see who could jump the most before they got picked up. I won. I got eighty-two and she got seventy-five. Did you see Parker get between us? Oh my god, he's always hanging around me. He's my son. Did you see me grab him and sling him around by his backpack? Ha ha! He kept spinning. I started jumping again but Emma didn't because she was laughing at Parker. So,I won, ha!"

Dwight smiled and said, "Emma and I. Yeah I saw you. You're lucky the line lady didn't see you, or I'd probably get another letter in the mail for a 'violent offense'."

She snorted as she put her backpack on the seat and buckled herself in. Last year, she had been sent out of a pep rally for being disruptive. The whole story was that she sort of slapped this girl in the side of the head. The girl had been threatening to hit her first. They weren't fighting, but the girl was beginning to annoy Abigail. She wouldn't get out of her face, so Abigail boxed her on the side of her ear once. The girl ran off and told on her, and they both got sent out of the pep rally, and it became a 'violent offense' on Abigail's permanent record. No one called them; they didn't send a note home from school, and Abigail never said anything about it. Dwight found out when Marlene opened a letter from the school about it four days later, and he started to march up to the school until she reminded him it was closed. Marlene told him she would call and talk to the principal the next day. She did, and the principal decided to knock it down from a 'violent offense' to 'horseplay' instead. Dwight just shook his head when Marlene told him that. If she hadn't called, it would still be a 'violent offense' on Abigail's record. That would look good when she applied to college, her being a violent offender in elementary school.

"Violent offense? What? Oh, when I hit Stacey last year because she wouldn't get out of my face? Well," she said pulling a bag of crackers out of her backpack, "she should've got out of my face when I warned her like fifty times."

As he drove, he watched her in the mirror, smiling. She was a lot like her mother. "Well just be careful. If someone messes with you too much just go tell on them I guess, so they won't take you to little kids' prison."

"They have prison for little kids? Wow that's cool. Do they get to watch TV and have recess and stuff? I want to go to little kids' prison. I should have hit her again."

Dwight laughed out loud.

"Turn on the tunes dad."

The rest of the way home she sang and directed him on changing the channels. They were home by 3:40, and Abigail got an apple and went outside in the backyard to play while Dwight got on the computer.

He was an avid gamer and his current other life was spent in the world of "World War III." It was an interactive online game for twenty players. Countries were randomly assigned on the first day of the game, and from 3:30 to 5:30 p.m. he played World War in real time for as long as it took for one side to destroy the other. Some games had lasted more than a year. There were no set treaties or sides, and it could be a total war of each man for himself, or he could form an alliance like those in the first two real world wars. It was a highly addictive game and had been compared to a drug. Players had lost their jobs and marriages over the game. Two people had heart attacks over the game, one while playing. Dwight wasn't as bad as all that; he just liked the game, and he was good at it. He had the tiny island of Japan this time and was currently allied with Russia; after three months, the rest of the world was beginning to suffer from this alliance. His counterpart who played Russia was some guy named Brian, a postman or something from Oregon. They communicated through headsets during the game and by texting and email a couple times a week to hash out long campaigns. Dwight thought Brian was a bit of a wuss in real life, but he was ruthless in the game. Only a well-worded treaty in the first week saved Dwight from being destroyed; after that he rode Brian's coattails and became equally powerful. The two of them had begun to scare the rest of the world, and Dwight kept his eye on new treaties being formed. He was pressuring Brian to tone it down until they were ready. Brian could have taken him out a few times but through an odd sense of loyalty to the treaty and maybe, a little fear of Japan's power, they had remained allies. Dwight secretly worked with Italy before they were crushed by Russia's army, and he had secrets of the A-bomb that he kept from Brian. Soon Japan would unleash death from the sky on the Russians, and he would assume total world dominance.

Today, however, Dwight was roaming the desert of Australia, looking for a band of British scientists trying to reach Mexico. They carried the secrets of some weapon, but his intel told him it was dangerous, and he pursued them with a slow relentlessness. He didn't think there was a Russian on the continent and he was going to get these secrets, and kill the scientists without causing a stir.

Then BOOM, Marlene was home.

"WHERE'S ABBY?"

She clomped in and landed her suitcase-sized purse down on the table with a bang. Marlene never really just came into a room, she bounded into it. She exploded into it, crushing and snuffing the life out of whatever was there before her. She grabbed it in her hands and shook it, and every action seemed to scream, "Wake up, I'm here!"

"Hi honey!" he said, all sarcasm. "She's in the backyard."

"NO. She is NOT."

It was one of those final things people said, like judges when they read your sentence, and you knew you really were going to jail for the rest of your life. A chill slipped into him and he let the game go, but he tossed the headset on the desk dramatically, so he could go find Abby up a tree or behind the lawnmower. Then he could give Marlene the look, but then he saw her face, a little puffy and tired and blanketed in worry. Dwight headed quickly past her pushing the screen door open and looked outside into the emptiness of the backyard, still and quiet. Even the surrounding yards had that feel of emptiness; a blind man would know no one was there. He glanced at the playground and looked up in the one tree she could climb, then he looked up into the trees she couldn't climb, and then he looked over into the neighbors' yards and felt his heart slide past his stomach and the pulse rise in his neck. After a few long seconds of searching his yard and the neighbor's yards, he didn't worry about the neighbors and he began to scream out loudly, "ABBY! ABBY!"

And just like that she was gone, and she was gone for two weeks. When they got her back she would be gone forever, and the knowledge of what happened to her during those two weeks was more than they could stand together. They came apart like two fighting lions, cutting deep and irreparable.

The funeral was painfully memorable in the drama that was Dwight when he got up to view Abby's open casket. His face was red and swollen, with both eyes squeezed near shut as he snuffled and shuffled his way to the casket. He would have had to crawl if his uncle had not been there. Marlene was in some lost room of the church with her sisters and mother, all blubbering. Anguished wails mixed with hushed voices wafted around the walls and filtered into Dwight's hearing during brief pauses in his own suffering, reminding him that he had let her get taken.

Now he was like a fighter beaten near to death and barely able to see. The large brown shape of the casket where she lay dead loomed in front of him like a spider, waiting for him to get closer. He could make out the open end and he edged toward it, approaching his own end because surely he was dying. As he neared, shapes and colors began to become clearer inside the casket, and Dwight was suddenly standing over her like he might have been at bedtime, getting ready to kiss her on her cheek, or maybe just coming to wake her up in the morning. He grasped the edge of the casket, hoping he would not stumble and pull it over. He felt alone suddenly, and realized his uncle had stepped back and was crying behind him. Dwight looked inside and focused on her dress. She was in a blue and red velvety dress that she had never owned. It was made and bought, to be worn one time only and forever. The bottom half of the casket was closed, and he could not see the rest of her. He felt cheated. *The last time I see her and I can't even see all of her?*

Dwight heard a little gasp and a murmur behind him as he realized he was lifting the closed end of the casket, but he did not stop. He gently let it rest open and looked down and saw her legs in white stockings. Her tiny feet were covered by blue shoes with little sparkly blue ribbons on the tops of them. Her small hands were folded over her belly and clasped together, and Dwight realized that somebody had done all of this. Someone had dressed her in a dress that had never been hers, put her in shoes that she had never worn, but would have loved, and then folded her arms and clasped her hands together. He had not looked at her face yet but he had been to funerals before with an open casket. It was usually older people with unnatural makeup, rosy cheeks, and powdered faces, and every time he had cringed a little. Dwight did not want to look at her. They typically looked like what they were, dead faces with makeup.
 He clenched the sides of the casket again in morbid, torturous fear. If they had painted her face in an unreal glaze, like she was a doll, a grotesque dead toy girl from China, he would probably come unloose. He heard his own rasping breath and felt the sweat under his arms and rolling down his back and he paused and closed his eyes. He leaned his head back slowly opening his eyes again to the ceiling. He felt his weight shift back, off balance. He held tightly to the casket, and with a vague panic thought he really might pull it down on top of himself. He heard nothing from behind him and nothing around him. Then suddenly, the sharp forceful voice of his wife came through to him and he straightened. She was

still in her lost room lamenting, cursing him probably, but there was no other sound. Dwight closed his eyes again and forced his head back down. He stilled himself and rested a moment as he heard a whisper from someone sitting behind him. He lowered his head slowly, opening his eyes, and finally looked at her face, the face he helped make. It was a beautiful, perfect face, and he saw the soft smooth and clean skin of his ten-year-old daughter, and felt the rest of his life fall out of him. She was unmarked by bruise or makeup, and this was much, much worse.

He started crying unabashedly now, and tears dropped on the white silk of the casket, on her velvet dress. He stared at her still face through waves of blurry tears, and he could not bear it anymore. He leaned in and scooped his arms under her gently and grabbed her to him, trying to bring her back. He squeezed her tightly and whispered in her ear, "I'm sorry Little Snail, oh honey, I'm sorry, Abigail, honey, I'm soooo sorry. I'm gonna come getcha real soon, Daddy will watch out for you. You wait for Daddy, you wait! Sorry, so sorry!"

He could only see white but he didn't know if he had his eyes open or closed, and then he began to feel a pain in his gut, and then a smell began to hit him. His face grew painfully hot against her cheek and he didn't know if he was still leaning over the casket holding her, or if he had pulled her out. *How long have I been standing here, and* what *is that smell?* It was as if a bomb had gone off in his stomach and he was all blown open. He almost doubled over but something stopped him, and he realized he was still holding Abby. Someone exclaim behind him, his uncle maybe, and now louder noises were around him. Then there were hands under his arms pulling at him.

Finally, through the confusion of it all, he heard one voice, Marlene. "STOP IT, STOP IT, STOP IT! PUT HER BACK, PUT HER BACK! WHAT ARE YOU DOING?" He felt her raging anger like bricks against his head, and her hands were scratching, clawing, and beating, and he knew they were falling. That was his last memory of Abigail's funeral.

CHAPTER 2

Dwight sat at the bar with one hand around his drink and the other holding a cigarette over the ashtray. He breathed in the stench of smoke and liquor, while the linger of perfume and deodorant suffocated the bar. It was like sustenance to him, and he let it back out slowly. With his eyes half closed, he pulled easy and slow on the cigarette and blew it out, watching the smoke billow as it jumbled in with all the odors.

He was at his bar, The Shame. Dwight didn't own it, but he was here enough to be part owner. He hadn't ordered a drink in here since the first week he came in. They learned to set one on the bar at 7:10 p.m.and he'd be at his stool and have his hand around it minute or two later. It took him less than a minute to drink it down and then there'd be another one one the bar before he was done. Dwight drank short doubles of vodka and coke. He usually stayed for about eight of them, then he'd put $60 on the bar, leaving around ten or eleven..

He came into The Shame Monday through Saturday, but on Saturdays he started about noon.

Saturday was his bad day. He sometimes got sent home in a cab, and he once spent the night at the police station. Around 8:00 or 9:00 pm, people from other bars or clubs began to roll in, and if one of them looked at him too long or bumped him trying to get a drink and didn't apologize, Dwight would get off his stool, and there would be a problem. He was an angry drunk late on Saturday evenings and the bartenders had to keep an eye on him. Dwight wanted to cause someone pain, someone who deserved it, and they usually showed up on Saturday nights.

He had been coming into The Shame for eight months now and had somehow grown on the bartenders and some of the regulars. Maybe it was just his consistency. Dwight hadn't said much that first day but he laid sixty dollars on the bar when he was done and said he would be back tomorrow at 7:10, and thank you. 'Okay bud,' Belly, the bartender and owner had said, not thinking much of it until he saw the three twenties. His bill was 48 dollars. Belly was impressed with the amount of vodka poured into him and had watched him as the night wore on, when he went to the bathroom, or lit a cigarette, and didn't notice any impaired movements until he finally got up to leave. The man rose slowly and steadied himself and then turned his head to locate the door before heading out. Eight short doubles. That was 16 shots of vodka in four hours. Except that Belly had begun to cheat him on the vodka after the fifth drink. He didn't want him slamming into a telephone pole when he left and then his have his long lost sister or other suing the bar.

The next day he came in and sat down in the same spot and asked loudly where his goddamn drink was. Belly cocked a look at him and began to tell him where his goddamn drink was when he said, "It's 7:10. I told you yesterday I'd be here at 7:10, now where's my motherfuckin' drink?", and then he smiled a sad disarming smile, and Belly relaxed. He hadn't caused any trouble yesterday and had brought 60 dollars into his bar on a Tuesday, which hadn't been doing much on the weekdays for the last year, with most of his customers laid off from the Chrysler plant. This guy had the look of a good fella who'd been kicked and then kicked again maybe, and Belly decided he was alright.

"Sorry bud, vodka and coke? Yeah, short double. I think I served more of those yesterday than I have in the past five years."

"Rum is for drinks with umbrellas in them. Vodka is for men."

Belly smiled. "Damn right, think I'll have one."

"Only if I buy it and it's a short double. Don't be a pussy."

Belly smiled again. The nuts on this guy.

And he'd been there almost every day since, except Sundays. The main bar itself where he sat was in a horseshoe, with the bartenders in the middle, and it had about 15 stools around it and this is where most of the regulars sat. There were eight or ten little tables scattered around, three pool tables, and an overflow bar connected to the side of the main one. In the event they were busy, it had about six more stools. Dwight usually sat three chairs from the end of the main bar near the bathroom.

The first Saturday Dwight spent at The Shame was a dandy. Belly had two bartenders, Joni and Karen, come in at 6 p.m.to work the bar on Saturday nights. He was there also, but only to socialize and keep an eye on things, or to help out if the girls got slammed, which still happened sometimes. This Saturday was mildly busy with about 20 people sitting at the bar, at the tables, or playing pool. Dwight had shown up at noon and Belly served him until the ladies came in and Belly got his first look at him getting drunk. His laugh was a bit louder and more frequent and his words began to drag, but he still seemed manageable. The ladies had taken over for him at 6 p.m.and Dwight had been openly surprised at the change in personnel. He gave Belly a pained look, and for a brief moment Belly thought there might be some sort of weird problem. But then it was gone and after a short time of silence, Dwight warmed up and began to pester them, and Belly had the impression they liked it.

"You want another one, hon'? What was you drinkin'?" Joni said to Dwight as he set his empty glass down. She was kind of short with long, thick, stringy hair that was still hanging on to some curls from probably Thursday. Dwight noticed she was looking him in the eye, and a smile eased from her mouth the longer he took to answer. She was cute ten years ago at thirty-ish, and she still had the look of fun to her face.

"When the glass is empty, I wanna 'nother one loaded and ready to go before this'n hits the bar." He tapped his glass down and gave his cigarette pack a little shake and one jumped up. He let the pack drop and grabbed the cigarette out before the pack hit the bar. He picked up a book of bar matches and folded one of the matches under the book and snapped it against the striker. He lit his cigarette and looked up to see both Joni and Karen smiling at him. He closed two fingers over the flame.

Karen looked at him, waiting, then said "Well genius, what are you drinking?" Joni, Belly and several of the nearby patrons laughed. Karen was short and a little skinny and had a her sandy blonde hair in a ponytail hanging out of the back of a baseball cap. She looked to be in her early thirties. One tall idiot sitting a few stools to the right of him, whom Dwight had been eying occasionally through the evening because he was so loud and stupid, guffawed the loudest. Dwight eased his head over in his direction and cast him a long slow glance and then turned his head back and peered over at Belly dramatically and said, "Belly, you bedder git these girls lined out."

"Short double, vodka and coke," Belly said.

"Short double, vodka and coke. Well, I can do that," Joni said.

By 9:30 pm, Dwight was pretty drunk and he had a numb ache in his belly. His stomach had been aching for weeks now, off and on, or maybe it had been months. He ignored it so he really wasn't sure.

The tall idiot was dominating the talk and continually raising the noise level at the bar, like he was a conductor at a performance where you had to yell and make wild gesticulations to get the musicians to perform. His volume and abrasiveness was beginning to wear on those sitting at the bar, especially Dwight, and some regulars had already left. He had some long lost buddy playing pool and he

hollered terribly funny things at him every now and
then, and they yucked loudly back and forth. There
were some people who came into a ba,r and after a
couple drinks and a couple hours, they felt like they
owned the place. This guy and his buddy were like
that, and it made Dwight mad. His little girlfriend,
surprisingly cute, had moused into a hole and sat by
quietly, nodding and fake laughing at the right spots
as he demonstrated his stupidness. He commented
on Joni's drink-making wondering if there was water
in the rum bottle because, you know, they were both
clear, and about what the smell was in the bar, and he
made suggestions as to what some of the stains on the
floor might be, and all in the form of a joke everyone
got.

Dwight mulled in his drink and nested down
into his stool at the bar, waiting patiently for his
tolerance to run out. He was drunk, but he would
still be able to get home if he stopped pretty soon. He
was annoyed this guy continued to hammer away at
the shell he had worked on since noon, like a roofer
banging away above your head while you're trying to
watch TV. He was about ready to leave, and that
made him mad, because he didn't want to leave. He'd
been watching Belly and the girls, and he could tell
they would be happy to see this guy leave, but
working in a bar they were obliged to suffer through
this kind of customer. But Dwight, he didn't have to.

The man finished saying something loudly
and laughed, slapping the bar. Dwight hadn't even
been paying much attention and had no idea what he
had just said, but he suddenly decided the time was
now, and he said loudly, "Why don't you shut the
fuck up?"

The bar simmered quickly to a silence.

He paused a bit and looked around and then said to Dwight, "What did you say?"

"Shut. the. fuck. up. You're annoying..." He motioned his hand over his head in a swooping circle, "...the whole bar." He was disappointed no one clapped.

"Hey, lighten the fuck up, buddy." He said as he walked slowly around the bar, and Dwight knew then that he didn't have any sand. That walk was too slow. "This is a bar, man, and if I've been a little loud and offended you then I'm really *fuckin'* sorry." He spread his hands wide dramatically. He looked toward the pool table to see if he'd been heard, and Dwight was happy to see the buddy coming over, carrying a pool stick.

He got a little bolder. "I'm soorrry you've been crying in your beer all night pouting like a baby. What the fuck happened, you finally catch your wife cheating on you?" He turned to smile at his buddy. Dwight could tell he was trying to work himself up for what was about to happen.

He and Marlene had been separated for a year and a half, since the funeral, and divorced for several months, he wasn't sure how long, but he knew she'd been seeing somebody before then. It wasn't cheating, they were done before the funeral, but it had been a punch in the gut. To lean on another man's shoulder, to lay in bed with someone else, after their daughter had been used and crushed like a paper cup, to *move on*. It disgusted him, and he still had random thoughts about killing them. But he would never let anyone bad mouth her, and now the loud mouth had said that. Well, it didn't really matter what he would have said.

He took his last step toward Dwight, and Dwight left the bar stool and smashed his fist into his open mouth. His head snapped back, he went up on his toes, and he looked like a drunken swan trying to fly backwards. A second later he fell on the floor onto his back with a loud thud. Dwight straightened up and eyeballed the buddy with the pool stick who was all of the sudden undecided what to do, but with everyone watching he mustered up some courage and advanced on Dwight. As he went to break the stick over his knee and maybe use both pieces as weapons or just look cool, Dwight kicked him in his raised knee and sent him back into the wall. He bounced off the wall and fell to the floor with mirrors and beer signs crashing around him.

Dwight was trying to figure out which one was going to get up first, but Belly arrived and Dwight turned quickly back to the bar and pulled a hundred dollar bill out of his wallet and put it under his glass. He held his hands up to Belly and took a step toward the door and then said, "Good night ladies," to Joni and Karen who were staring at him. Dwight kept his head down as he turned to leave, and then he put his boot into the shoulder of the loud mouth as he was getting up and kicked him back down, and his head clanged off the side of a stool. He gave a crooked smile to Belly who said, "Hey!" and he walked to the door. Joni still held a drink in one hand and had her other hand over her open mouth. Karen had a big smile on her face and piped out, "Bye Dwight! See you next Saturday!" and she let out a loud cackling laugh. As fast as he could walk without falling over, Dwight was out the door, into his truck, and down the street before anyone else left the bar.

CHAPTER 3

A few weeks later Dwight was sitting on the toilet feeling his legs go numb. He was waiting for a giant poop, diarrhea, or a weird little animal to come rolling out. His stomach had been aching forever it seemed, and it wasn't going away. He really didn't know when it had started, but it was so constant now he was beginning to wonder what it was. Lately, it felt like cramps or nausea, with spastic shooting pains sometimes. At work it was somewhat dimmed though, maybe because he had something else to concentrate on besides dying. He was a "Cleaning Associate" in a large office complex downtown from 9:45am to 6:45pm. They were understaffed and while his other "associates" complained, Dwight worked, and there was enough to do to keep him busy all day, otherwise he would not have made it. After work, he went home to change, and then he was at The Shame until he was drunk enough, and the pain was dulled enough, so he could get some fast food and go home and go to sleep.

He thought about it as he sat on the pot and he tried to trace it back. There was a time back there that he didn't remember much of, and he tried never to think about, but now he remembered when he began to emerge from the dazed nightmare that was her disappearance, her murder, and her funeral, that he had started to feel a pain in his stomach. Dwight thought it was grief, and he did not deny it; he did not want it to leave. But now it was getting worse and it was beginning to affect his life like a kidney stone or something, and he wondered if there was something really wrong. Maybe he developed a swollen gland or strained a muscle with the stress of it all. It ached constantly and began to consume his thoughts. When he woke in the morning the ache was there and was always starting to be there somewhere deep in his gut, like a punch in the belly and a stomach ache all at different times. He thought a jagged piece of metal must be lost in there somewhere.

Nothing wanted to come out so Dwight got up and put his uniform on and sat on the bed to put on his shoes, but laid on his back instead. A few minutes later the alarm on his phone went off waking him up, reminding him to go to work. He put his shoes on and left.

Later that evening, he sat on his bar stool trying not to think. It was 8 p.m. on Thursday, and he was at The Shame, just beginning to feel okay for the day, when a couple walked into the bar talking and sat down a few stools from him. His hand crept to his stomach as he listened to them enter.

"...and he's my buddy, she's fine. He watched her before. He's only five blocks away."

"I don't like that goddamn van of his," the woman said. "Looks like a rape van."

Dwight's head came up and his face caught the woman's face as she sat down, and he felt a sharp piercing pain in his stomach. He grunted loudly and doubled over with the pain, and his forehead hit the bar. His head bounced back, and he pushed back in his stool. Before he could stop himself, he was falling backward with the stool, trying to right himself. He landed with his head at his knees, crashing into a sitting position on top of the fallen stool. Dwight stumbled over the side as he tried to maintain his balance, but the pain was an intense cramp that would not allow him to straighten up. He fell over on his side in a loud heap. Belly came quickly around the bar and grabbed his flailing hand, trying to help him up.

"No! No!" Dwight grimaced and remained hunched over on one knee

"Buddy are you okay? What happened man, you sick? You need a doctor?" Belly asked.

Dwight panted for a second, trying to work up the ability to say he just had a bad cramp when the man walked up and loomed over Dwight.

"Are you alright?"

Dwight felt him and smelled him. The smell coming off him was familiar, but was so nauseating he couldn't focus. The pain spiked in his stomach like a porcupine flexing its quills. He yelled out and put his hand up to ward him off, and the man stopped in confusion.

"I'm okay" Dwight stammered barely, praying he didn't come any closer. "Bad cramp," he managed, trying not to vomit. "I'm okay. Thanks, go sit down, go sit down." He waved his hand at him and bade him sit down. Belly helped him up, staring at him.

"I'm gonna go, okay? I'll be back tomorrow, yeah?"

"Yeah. Yeah sure man, yeah it's okay. Are you okay? Do you need an ambulance? I mean, can you make it home?"

The man had made his way back to his seat and was whispering to his wife.

Dwight slowly eased himself straight, still leaning on Belly. His gut clenched and unclenched, but he felt he could make it to the door. After that he would crawl. He had to get away from this dude.

"I'm okay, something I ate." He said, though he hadn't eaten since lunch at 11:30. He hobbled toward the door, not thinking about or looking at the couple, knowing they stared at him as he walked out. He could feel them though, and he knew if he looked their direction he would not make the door. The scent hung in the air around them, like vomit, or sewer. There was something wrong with those two, and Dwight had to get away from the smell or he would collapse. He shoved himself through the door and felt the chill outside, saw the darkness of the night, and turned around and pushed the bar door closed. He leaned against it with one hand gripping the skin of his stomach. It throbbed like a massive pimple, and he wanted to jab a knife into it.

He made it to his truck panting and crying a little now. Crying more from fear and loneliness than pain. He missed his daughter. He missed his wife. He missed his life, and he wanted to die. It was a vagrant thought he'd been having lately, dying.

Dwight realized one day at work as he mopped the

23

main lobby, that he'd been thinking about dying for the last two hours, in a sort of casual way, feeling with some shock that he was on his way to committing suicide. He had nothing. There was mind-numbing work, drinking to smother the memories and the pain, and sleeping. He raised his head up over the steering wheel and looked into the parking lot of The Shame. There were four cars other than his. Belly's old Mercedes, Tom's '84 ford truck, an old Grenada that had been abandoned weeks ago that Belly let sit because it looked like he had customers, and then what must be the couple's car. It was a purple four-door Saturn of some sort. Dwight looked at it. It looked menacing under the dim illumination of the one overhead light in the parking lot, like it was looking at him. He stared at it until the pain began to knot in his insides again. He started his truck up and put it slowly in gear. *I should do it tonight.*

He pulled up to the street and stopped. The pain throbbed like the porcupine had settled in to sleep, the quills stabbing in and out as it breathed. *What the fuck is wrong with me? It's probably cancer or a tumor; well I'm not going to the goddamn doctor.* He turned the wheel to the right, towards his home, and pulled out on the street. The pain abated and a block away from the bar it was almost gone. Dwight stopped the truck in the street. He sat there idling, wondering. He checked the rearview for traffic and turned the truck around. He drove slowly back down the street and approached the bar. He waited for it to come. He felt a little prick, just a little rumble, and then he rounded the curve in the road and rolled on down the street.

He relaxed his grip on the steering wheel and let his right hand slip onto his lap.

"What the fuck..."

He idled slowly down the street just driving, passing the parked cars in their driveways, with their trees and their lawns and their families, lit by porch lights and dim street lights. He rolled the windows down and let the night air in and he suddenly had a memory of Abby when she was about two years old. They had a tiny little 3 inch step down between the laundry room and the back sunroom. Dwight had been in the sunroom cleaning the mud off his boots when she appeared in the doorway dressed in some little blue jeans, a cute "I'm a Real Terror" t-shirt, and those little bitty kid shoes.

"Hi Abby Snail. Whachoo doin' Honey?"

She stood on the precipice of the giant 3 inch step and peered down at the lower floor of the sun room. Abby looked up at him with determination and then jumped off the little step. He started to say something mild like "wow, very nice." But then this smile appeared on her face, stretching from ear to ear and showing all her perfect tiny white teeth. Her face glowed like a star, her eyes sparkled, and he knew he could not just simply congratulate this feat. She had really done something.

"OH MY GOSH! ABBY! WOW that was fantastic!" And she *beamed* at him. She *had* done something amazing. She went back and climbed deliberately up the little step and turned around. She looked at her daddy, and without looking at the floor jumped again, and the same pure happiness of a smile spread across her face. Dwight looked at her and felt a gush of love people are so unaccustomed to, and he cheered wildly for her again, and again and again. He did not tire of this event like he did so many of her other miracles as she grew older. He was a good father that day.

He raised his right hand in a fist and slammed it on the dash of the truck again and again screaming, "NO NO NO NO!". Then he went quiet and still, driving automatically, hating himself. His mind was as dark as his heart and somewhere inside one of them, the decision was made. There was no more hope, no more love, no more point.

He kept driving with the night wind swirling gently inside the truck, and then the smell floated in faintly for one quick moment and rammed itself up his nose like a needle, then pulled out and was gone. He stopped the truck and blinked his eyes and then rolled both windows down all the way. He braced himself, and smelled. Dwight sifted through the air like a miner, searching. He filtered the long breath of air and found nothing, then exhaled and inhaled again, slowly, listening with his nose but finding nothing. He stuck his head out the window and breathed in again and found it faintly, but sharp and nasty. He pulled his head back in the truck, and rubbed his eyes. Then he leaned his head back out of the window and looked to his left back down the street at the houses on the left side.

It was a lower-class neighborhood, older cars were in the driveways and on the street. A car was parked up on the grass of one house, with a cinder block holding up a missing wheel. Further down was one house with no cars in the driveway and none on the street in front. He looked at the house closer. He did see a vehicle there, but it was up in the carport

attached to the side of the house. It looked like a van.
The words of the couple in the bar came back to him.
She had said his buddy's van looked like a rape van,
and he said he only lived a few blocks from the bar.
Dwight put the truck in drive and went to the next
intersection and took a left. He made two more lefts
around the block and eased up quietly to the curb in
front of the house. He could see more of the van. It
was a green van, one of the full-size ones but the
short version. It was dirty green in color with rust
showing at the bottom. He noticed it didn't have any
windows on the sides or the back, just the in the front
driver and he assumed the passenger side. A "rape
van" his wife also would have called it. His ex wife.
The kind of van guys who kidnapped people and
raped them drove around in. Dwight looked quickly
at the house and stared at it like it might show him
something. He felt the knot in his stomach curl up
and tighten into a small burning mass in the pit of his
belly. He rolled the window down and the smell
hung just outside like the smell of human waste hangs
inside the door of a bathroom. He wondered what he
was going to do as he opened the door of his truck
and put one foot out on the curb. Then he heard
something faint like a muted yelp coming from the
house, and to his surprise he was in the grass and
shutting the door softly. He crept quickly up the
driveway and past the carport, which seemed to be
full of boxes, a motorcycle, and some other junk.
The side of the house was dark and the backyard was
fenced, but the gate was cracked open, which meant
no dog. He slipped through the gate with a little
creak and paused. Light from the house escaped
through the windows and shed light on the back yard.

He stepped into the back yard a few feet and noticed
the area beneath his feet and out into the yard a ways
was only dirt. He peered into the dark corners of the
yard, and noticed a curved arc the dirt made in the
grass, the arc a dog makes walking to the limits of its
chain, and now Dwight wondered about a dog. Then
he heard the slow pull of a chain being dragged over
wood, and he froze.

A large, skinny, scarred-up, mean-looking dog
was emerging slowly from the dark shadow of a dog
house, and Dwight knew that dog would eat him. If
it couldn't get to him and eat him, it would certainly
bark. He didn't move. He watched as the dog
walked slowly toward him and then stop before it
reached the end of the chain. It stood looking at
Dwight but made no threat nor did it wag its tail. The
dog suddenly looked toward the house with his ears
cocked, but Dwight heard nothing. He breathed out
softly, "Hey buddy…" and eased slowly toward the
back door with the dog looking at him. If it was
going to eat him, it would have probably done it by
now. He let out a breath and carefully made his way
to the back door, watching the dog with his ears keen
for a sound, expecting the rush of teeth up his butt.
The house smelled of vomit and refuse, the knot
gurgled and churned. He ducked under a window
and approached the door. There was a storm door
but the screen and glass were missing. The back door
was white and stained with mud. He grasped the
knob and held still, listening, and heard the noise he
realized he was listening for. There was a small sound
inside the house like something had fallen on the
floor and a short burst of muffled talking that quickly
subsided. Dwight turned the knob and found it

unlocked. With a dog like that, who locks the door?
He pushed it open and stepped quietly into the house,
into a little kitchen with old yellow vinyl floors and
painful looking white cabinets, with a scarred yellow
countertop. There was a little round table with two
chairs and an ashtray, complete with burning
cigarette, a beer can, a cup of milk and a plate of
uneaten fish sticks and ketchup. The house reeked of
the smell. Dwight's eyes watered and bile rose in his
throat.

He heard a little whimper from a child down
the hallway, and then crying, and he was at once
resolved, thinking if this was just a dad getting onto
his kid, he would apologize, saying he was just
walking by, and he heard a noise or something and
run off. He went silently through the kitchen and
down the hall and stopped to listen at a partially
closed door. He heard a man say it would be okay,
that no one would know, and Dwight's temper hit the
roof and he banged the bathroom door open. The
smell was in the bathroom like a gas leak. A girl of
nine or ten was sitting on the sink and she started
with a little squeal. A toothbrush vase was lying
broken on the floor. The man turned quickly, and
Dwight saw his pants undone. His hand jerked away
from her leg and the three of them froze for a
moment. In that long moment Dwight took in his
open pants and saw the nasty mess of pubic hair and
the bulge below the partially undone zipper. She had
red lipstick not put on very well and the top button
on her shorts was undone and her shirt was partially
tucked in, like he had been digging in her shorts.
Dwight's head filled with heat and he felt the volcanic
eruption of his rage. The intense sadness, loss, and

grief for his perfect little daughter all exploded inside of him. All of this took a moment, and before the man could even begin to protest, Dwight released it all upon him, from his failure to protect her, from what he knew was done to her but he never let himself think of, and he grabbed him by the neck with both hands and slammed his head into the wall, then jerked him away from the sink and the girl and drove him into the bathtub head first. He pushed him on his back into the tub and pounded on his face again and again with his right hand. He was faintly aware that he was yelling. The man flailed and grunted but was soon unable to defend himself and he lay there as Dwight beat on him until the pain in his hand forced him to stop. He hovered over the man, gasping, panting, hating, watching him for signs of life, when he heard a sound from the girl. She was still in the bathroom. He didn't turn around but said in a ragged voice, "Go in the kitchen."

He waited a few moments panting and staring at the man until he saw him sputter for life. Dwight wanted to choke him to death, choke him until his hands squeezed through his neck and his head popped off, but his hand hurt too much. He slid him all the way into the tub and stomped his boot onto his face a few times. The sound made him sick and the smell was beginning to make him dizzy. He moved his head with his boot and stepped onto his throat, putting all of his weight on that one boot, and he stood on his neck. He held it there for a long while, until he felt sure. He stepped back weakly from the tub and looked down at him. His chest, his eyes, nor his mouth, nothing moved. He steadied himself against the sink. He looked at his hand, red with blood and thick and swollen, and he looked at the blood he had dripped onto the sink. He got a towel and wiped off the sink and wrapped it around his hand. He wiped at a few blood smears on the wall and shower curtain. He thought briefly about all the ways he could be linked to what had just done, his DNA and blood all over the place. Marlene loved real crime shows where the guy was caught because there was a tiny leaf in the trunk of his Pinto with a minute drop of blood on the back of it, and Dwight didn't hold out much hope for himself. Surely some of his blood was on this guys face. The rest of the bathroom seemed okay but probably wasn't. He had to leave. He turned the shower on hot and washed his hands and some of the curtain off, then watched as it splattered on the man's body, soaking his clothes and washing his face, and then he shut the curtain.

Dwight walked back through the house and found her sitting at the kitchen table with her head down, sobbing and shaking. Her head came up sharply when he entered, and her face was a miserable look of shame and fear. She didn't look ten anymore and when she saw him she bawled up and began crying loudly, backing away.

"Oh no, Honey, no, no. It's not your fault; it's not your fault. He was a bad man, right? What he was doing was wrong. No one is supposed to do that to you. But I fixed him, okay?. He won't hurt you no more, Honey." She was looking at him through huge red and swollen eyes, tears all over her face, and she buried her head in her lap and covered it with her arms. The need to protect her, to grab her and run off somewhere safe was almost overwhelming. His head throbbed and he could hear his own pulse banging in his ears. He suddenly grabbed her up and held her, squeezing her wretched sobs against him. After a few moments, when she wasn't calming down, he realized she was probably crying as much over what he had done and him standing there holding her as anything else, but he kept hugging her and petting her and shooshing her. After several minutes she began to settle a little and he set her back down. He brushed her hair back and wiped her face with a paper towel.

"You believe in God, Honey?"

She didn't seem to understand at first but after a few seconds nodded her head slowly.

"Good. That's right."

He paused and motioned with his toweled hand to the bathroom. "God knew what he was doing, okay, and He told me to come stop him. Okay? It was wrong. He was wrong." He nodded his head at her. What in the hell am I doing, he thought. *What the fuck have I done?* She looked slowly away from him and stared at the floor.

Dwight looked at the kitchen wall, amazed to see a phone hanging on it. He grabbed the phone with the paper towel and hit 911, and then hung up. He didn't know the address. He doubted she knew. He didn't even know what street he was on. He hit redial and waited.

"911 what is your emergency?"

"There's been a man killed, um… he was…ah doing something he shouldn't have been with a little girl. How long will it take you to trace this call?"

"Sir I have a trace on you now, 305 West Walnut? Who was killed? Are you sure he's dead?"

"She's still here and I'm, uh…going to leave. He was molesting her…so I…uh...you'll have to ask her about what he was doing, he's in the bathroom, and she's in the kitchen." He hung up.

He turned to her. She was breathing heavily, but was otherwise still, just staring at the floor. He thought she was probably in shock. "Don't go in the bathroom, okay? Don't go in there, and he can't come out, okay? He's done, he's not coming back out, okay? He's never coming back out. You'll be fine in here for a few minutes until the police get here. What's your name?"

"Kayla." She said softly after a moment.

"Do you know where your mom and dad are?"

She shook her head after another moment.

"They told you they were at The Shame didn't they? They're at The Shame bar, just down the road." He pointed. "The police will be here soon. Do you like fish sticks?"

She bowed her head and began to cry again. He bent and kissed her on the head and said, "Okay, Honey. Don't eat the fish sticks. Nobody likes fish sticks, they're gross, right? Okay, you'll be okay." *Oh my god, can I fuck this up more?*

He grabbed a dish rag off the counter and opened the back door with it. He paused and said to her back, "Your parents are at the bar down the street, The Shame. None of this was your fault." Then he shut the door behind him and wiped off the knob. He found the dog had moved closer to the house but was still a few feet away and he hugged the side of the house as he left the backyard. As Dwight went through the gate, he heard a short bark and nearly fell over. He stopped and stuck his head back through the gate. The dog advanced steadily but cautiously. Dwight could see he was a brown boxer, but with some grey. He had white feet and a white slash between his eyes. The dog was big, about seventy pounds, with taught skin pulled over muscles and ribs, and a short nubby tail. He reached the end of his chain and gave a little whine. Dwight thought of police nearby getting the call, cutting tight corners and flicking on their lights. He imagined one doing a routine drive by of The Shame, headed this way right now.

He walked back into the yard and approached the big dog cautiously. He put his hands up slowly to the dog's nose, and the dog sniffed the towel wrapped around his hand. It sniffed the other hand quickly, then went back to the toweled hand, sniffing. Dwight relaxed and undid the leather collar with one hand, while the dog checked the rest of him out. The collar was nasty with dirt and age. The chain and collar felt to the ground, and Dwight looked at it for a moment, thinking. He pulled out his knife with his left hand and began trying to cut the collar loose from the chain with his broken hand. The dog nosed his way in and sniffed the collar furiously. "Move dog," Dwight whispered. He finally cut it loose and stuffed it in his pocket. Maybe they'd think the dog got loose chasing him. He hustled through the gate and out to his truck, painfully aware of how bright it was with street lights and porch lights on here and there. He opened his door and was suddenly bumped against it as the dog pushed passed him and jumped into the truck. Dwight watched the dog look around in the truck sniffing stuff, and then sit down in the seat against the passenger door. He sniffed the dash and the window, then looked at Dwight. Dwight didn't have time to worry about getting him out, so he got in. The street was on an incline and he struggled putting it in neutral with his left hand. The truck began to roll backward. He let it roll into the intersection and backed into the cross street. He stopped and then started the truck and put it into drive and he headed towards home with the dog looking through the windshield.

Ten minutes later, Dwight pulled into his driveway and parked. He looked over at the dog sitting up in the seat looking out the windows. He wondered about what he had just done, and what to do now. His hand throbbed, and he thought it might be broken in a few places. The towel with the man's blood and his blood was stuck to his skin. He would need a cast. If he went to the ER now the police might run checks on people admitted tonight. He didn't know how they did that, but he was tired and didn't want to go anyway. Although Tuesday night was probably a good night to go, not too busy maybe. *Aw fuck it.*

"C'mon, dog, get out."

He got out and the dog pushed by him, quickly on the ground sniffing and snorting around the yard.

"Scuse me dog."

The dog raised his leg and marked a few places. Dwight went to the front door and opened it looking at the dog who was now by his side looking up at him. Without further discussion, the dog went inside. Dwight followed him in and went to the kitchen. He got a beer and took two of the pills left

over from his breakdown and downed them with half
of the beer. He cleaned his hand off under the cold
water of the kitchen tap. He got a second beer and sat
in the dark on the couch, while the dog walked
around and sniffed everything he owned. He stared
through the slits of the mini-blinds out onto the
empty street, thinking about it but trying not to think
about it. Adrenaline seemed to be coursing aimlessly
through him, looking for something else to do. He
sat unmoving, just staring out the window while the
dog made noises as it searched the house. He took in
a deep breath in and let it out. He felt okay for the
first time since she went missing. A small amount of
peace was on him. And that damn pain in his
stomach was gone.

CHAPTER 4

He got the cast on Wednesday afternoon at a full service clinic without much fuss and went home and slept the rest of the day. He was off for the rest of the week with the broken hand, and he was supposed to be off for two weeks but he told them he'd be back on Monday, and would be able to do all of his duties even with the cast. His boss seemed put out and said, "A bar fight?" twice like he'd never heard of people fighting in a bar and he said they'd talk when he came in on Monday. It was going to be a short-lived talk though. Most talks with Dwight were tight and strained. He was a janitor anyway. People nodded and smiled at him as they stepped on the floor he was mopping.

He took the dog with him Thursday to the hardware store and got some supplies to fix the holes in fence. It wasn't his house; he rented it, and he didn't think he was even supposed to have pets but he didn't care. His landlord knew something about him and didn't bother him. Dwight had forgotten to pay rent for almost two months, and when he called to apologize and pay the late fees, the landlord had acted like it was no big deal. His landlord was a pretty good guy.

Dwight muddled through the fence repair most of the day Thursday with his broken hand and the dog shoving his nose in everywhere. He didn't think he really needed the fence. The dog didn't seem to be going anywhere. He was a handsome dog except for being skinny. He had some scars on his head, like scratches or bites from fighting, and a four inch long line on his upper shoulder. Dwight thought his now dead owner may have been into dog fighting. "He was into lots of things he don't do anymore, huh dog." The dog shoved his head into Dwight's way as he tried to bend down and tighten a nut. "God damn, move your big ass head." The dog wagged his nubby tail and kept helping.

They got the fence done, good enough anyway, and he loaded the dog up and took him to the vet. Dwight had a moment of fear when the vet picked up a scanner looking device, as he suddenly remembered some animals had tracking chips in their necks. He waved the scanner over the dog's neck and no beep sounded and Dwight relaxed. That loser never took this dog to the vet, he thought. Dwight told them he'd found the dog by his house. The vet told him the dog was about two years old but was not full blood Boxer. He noticed the scars and gave Dwight a look, but not of suspicion.

"I bet this guy broke loose from his previous owner. He was probably fighting him." The vet said. Dog agreed with whatever the vet said as he sat still and looked at them seriously. "This is a good dog though. Besides underfed and a little mistreated he seems very friendly. And good looking! Look at the muscles on him. I bet you didn't lose too many fights, huh? What's his name?"

"Uh…" Dwight said stupidly. He hadn't thought the dog needed a name, he'd been thinking of him as Dog. "Dog, I guess."

"Ha! Dog, just like the John Wayne movie. Have you seen that one?" Dwight shook his head no. "He's out riding around being a cowboy, being John Wayne you know, and he's got this dog along with him and he just calls him Dog the whole time." Dwight thought that sounded about right.

He got home and got Dog all fixed up in the back yard with a big plastic dog house and water and food. He had a time carrying the dog house with one hand, but he got it situated by the back door and gestured for Dog to get in it, but he just stood there, looking, so Dwight let it be. "I bet you get your ass in there when it rains."

He discovered it was about 4:30 and he'd run out of things to do so he left Dog in the backyard and headed for The Shame. When he got there, he sat in his truck in the parking lot looking at the door. There was a strange vehicle in the lot besides Belly's and the Grenada. It didn't really mean much, unless you considered what he'd done after the last time he'd left here.

He finally got out and walked in and he could at first see no one in the bar at all. He sat down on his stool letting his eyes adjust and he heard talking, and then he noticed Belly sitting at a table with a young woman, talking earnestly. Belly seemed to be explaining something to her, and she appeared to be crying a little. Dwight wished he'd come in an hour later. He lit a cigarette and went to look at the pictures on the wall. There was a collection of them on a bulletin board showing the celebration of The Shame's tenth year. There had been quite a crowd that night. The Shame was one of those dives everyone loved to go to occasionally. Some bars just have the right feel. Dwight liked it because most of the time it was just regulars but there was enough of a mix of regulars and others especially on Friday and Saturday to keep it from being stale. He finally found Joni in the pictures; she had died blonde hair then. She was a fun-loving girl. There was one of her on Belly's shoulders, facing the way other than normal holding on to the back of his head, and she had a big smile on her open mouth. He looked for a date and finally found one that had a date stamp. Belly had been in business for 15 years. Wow, he thought, Joni had been tending bar here for at least 5 years.

He heard a glass clink and ice rattle and turned and saw Belly at the bar so he made his way back over to his stool. Belly had a look on his face like he might make on the toilet. He set Dwight's drink down and held up the soda/water dispenser.

"This is the button for coke and I'll put the bottle right here by you…if you don't mind getting your own for a minute?"

"Yeah sure man." Belly nodded and quickly returned to the table.

Dwight grabbed the drink and savored the moment before drinking it, putting the glass up to his lips and smelling the alcohol in the drink as the bubbles popped under his nose. He opened his mouth tilted the glass and poured the sweet, laced drink in slowly but steadily, drinking it all. He felt the sting of the alcohol and the sting of the carbonation as he put the glass down. He ran his tongue over his teeth getting the drink off them. Dwight sighed deeply. Then he leaned over the bar and made himself another one, trying to make it exactly like Belly had made the first one. He settled into his drink,his stool, and his cigarette and breathed in the air of the bar. He tuned his ears towards Belly's table as he looked at the various pictures and beer signs.

They were far enough away not to be clearly heard, but Belly was excited and raised his voice on occasion and Dwight heard; "…a fucking loser! And if he ever…Told you not to…" and on and on. Belly spoke most of the time and she cried and wiped her face. Dwight decided she was his daughter, and she was caught up with some guy who beat her, cheated on her, or sat on the couch and stole her money and then kicked her out, or all of that. Dwight thought most guys today *were* losers.

In his life before, he had worked as a bricklayer for 9 years, in a trade of men, and he was generally disgusted with most of them. They cheated on their wives and openly talked about it at work, like they dared anyone to snitch on them. They lied to each other. They sucked up to the boss when he was around and then talked about him when he wasn't. They tried every way possible to get out of work and get more money for doing it. They stole from the site, from the customer, and from the company. They lied to the government to get out of taxes and told each other how they did it, like they were explaining how to take out a carburetor or something. This guy named Jesse once had everyone in a circle explaining how he fixed the odometer on his truck so it wasn't keeping track of the miles. He said he was going to keep it that way for a couple years or something. That way, when he traded it in it he would get more money for it than it was worth.

Dwight pointed out this only cheats the next guy buying it from the lot. There was a short silent pause as they looked at him, and then someone asked for more details on exactly how to do it and they kind of shuffled him out of the circle. They had no respect. He wondered how anything got done.

He was working on his fourth drink when the door opened and a young couple came in, and he realized it was after dark when no light came in with the open door. They were mid twenties and the girl was good looking, like one of those 50's movie stars. She was modern and young but she had that adult, sophisticated look. Dwight noticed that he was pretty sharp too, and they seemed to protect each other, looking around the bar, pulling out stools and moving ash trays over. Dwight looked over at Belly who was still involved with his daughter and he got up and walked around the bar. He looked at them and smiled. "Let me guess, strawberry milk and a root beer float." She smiled warmly and looked around the bar, waiting for her man to handle the drink order and Dwight liked her immediately. The young man glanced at Dwight's drink over by his stool and asked, "What are you drinking?", pointing out that Dwight was not the bartender.

"Vodka and coke," he said affably.

The man looked at Greta Garbo for consent and she smiled and he said, "Two of those please, sir."

"One with a cherry," she said.

Dwight paused at that. Did they have cherries here? He looked around to find the bulk of Belly rounding the bar. Belly reached into a plastic bin and pulled out a cherry. He iced a glass and plopped the cherry in as Dwight moved back to his stool. Belly finished their drinks and collected the money, and then he made up Dwight another short double, gave him a nod as he set it down in front of him and he went back to the table.

Dwight looked over at them and the girl smiled again as did the man.

"What are you young spies up to tonight?"

The guy picked up his drink and made his way around one seat from Dwight and to Dwight's surprise she came around herself and sat in that chair in between them.

"We heard," she said secretively, "that this was the place to hire a hitman." She scanned the empty bar. Dwight laughed within himself, for the first time in months.

He leaned over to her cautiously and said, "Who you aimin' to kill? The fella next to you looks like a likely candidate." Dwight gave him a serious stare.

"No. Not him, not yet." She gave her man a placating smile then leaned into Dwight. "Not until we're married." And she rubbed her fingers together to indicate he had money. "But his mother…she is in *serious* need of killin'."

Dwight laughed out loud. "Oh shit man. Where did you luck into this girl?"

"I won her in a poker game," he said flatly. "But I'm not sure *won* is the right word." Then he said contemplatively, "Got cheated? The old bait and switch? Slight of hand maybe? I dunno."

Dwight sat there and chatted with them and he forgot about Belly. He made his drinks and he made their drinks and he didn't keep count. It was a very slow night, almost special in its lack of filler people. Belly was busy, and Dwight enjoyed the company of the spicy duo for the next two hours. They all got pleasantly drunk. Belly came over once for a drink for himself and his daughter, and later Dwight got them another, as he was basically the back up bartender.

But then three people came in, then two more, then a handful, and it turned lively and loud in his little bar. It put Dwight in a sour mood as it was getting harder to hear them and they started talking more to themselves. Then she turned to him and grabbed his arm with her warm hand and they said their goodbyes and the young man paid, and abruptly they left. Dwight felt like his only friends had abandoned him and he sulked for awhile. Belly had left his daughter at the table and was tending bar. She left soon after, and Belly was not talking. Dwight looked around gloomily and decided he'd had enough. He called Belly over.

"I'm not sure what I owe for leaving the other night." He put a hundred on the bar and nodded to Belly.

Belly picked the bill up. "No Dwight, we're okay." He handed it back to Dwight. "I got the other day and tonight. Thank you." Belly said and he held the bill out to him. "You okay?" He glanced at Dwight's cast as if for the first time but didn't remark on it. "You seem okay. Was it something you ate?"

Belly peered at him. He'd had a good day today, the best since when, and he realized he'd had no pains in his gut since that night. Something seemed unchained in him. Maybe he'd repaid his debt to Abigail. He teared up inside with the thought of her and struggled to shut it back down.

He took the hundred quickly and said, ""kay, Belly, see you tomorrow." Belly nodded and he left.

CHAPTER 5

On Saturday, Dwight got drunk and smacked two little gangster thugs around at the bar. They'd been beating him at pool, bouncing around like they owned the place as they tried to hold up their pants. He got tired of their smugness, and he was playing terrible pool. He was betting like an idiot too, and it also looked like one would distract him and the other would move the balls but he couldn't be sure. It hadn't taken much after that. He accused them of cheating and told them to put fifty dollars back on the table and to get the fuck out. They tried to box him in the corner and take him together but they didn't get very far. Belly heard raised voices and knew there was about to be a fight and got there just after it started. Dwight hit the one on the left in the face with his left hand and then immediately head butted the other one and they both went down. Belly pushed Dwight out of the way and told them to get out as they got to their feet. They tried to protest but

Belly told them, "Yeah two on one, I saw it. Get out and the cops don't get called."

"Wait outside if you want, girls. I'll be there after I finish my drink," Dwight said agreeably.

Belly gave him an angry look and said, "No, no. No he won't. Go on unless you want your warrants checked."

They left saying they would be waiting outside if he wasn't scared. Belly made Dwight sit at the bar with coke and no vodka and told him not to leave. Dwight flexed his left hand and sipped his coke, feeling the alcohol buzz around in his brain. Karen finished a drink order on the other side of the bar and came over to him smiling. He tried to straighten up, wondering what his hair looked like, but he didn't have any idea since he rarely looked at it.

"Well Rocky, didja win?", she said with a huge smile. She had one hand on the bar not too far from his and the other one on her hip. She had on a tank top and he found himself staring at her collarbone.

He felt his neck get hot and he cleared his throat before saying, "Well, I'm pretty sure they were cheating." He shrugged his shoulders.

"Yeah? So you beat them up?"

"Well, no, uh, I told them, all they had to do was leave the money on the table." He knew he sounded stupid.

"But they didn't wanna give that money up huh? Did you break your other hand? Lemme see."

She reached her hand out and grabbed his left hand and looked at his knuckles. Her hands were warm and soft. She pressed on his knuckles and he winced.

"Ow!"

"Oh! Sorry! Sorry! Is it broke? It's not broke. Are you okay? Big baby," she said letting his hand go and walking off with a jingling laugh.

He flexed his fingers thinking about her hands and smiled to himself. He sat there for another twenty minutes. No one was serving him anything, and the bar went back to its business. He watched Karen while trying not to stare as she zipped around the bar seeming to talk with everyone. She did twice the work Joni did even though Joni was usually busy, but they worked well together and he thought Karen wouldn't have worked any other way. She looked his way a few times and smiled, catching him looking. He didn't like to get caught but she was quicker than he was. He wasn't very good at this game. He finally decided he should go. He put his money on the bar under his glass and walked quietly out of the bar.

On his way home he went through the drive through at White Castle. He stuffed down six of the eight sliders before he got home. Though he wanted the other two, he saved them for Dog. He set them on the floor, not bothering with a plate. He knew Dog would lick the floor clean. Dog ate the two little burgers and looked at Dwight with a face that said 'you can put the rest down now, I'm ready'.

"You're lucky I didn't eat those you fat fuck. Shut up man, there's still dog food in your bowl."

Dwight went into his room and kicked off his shoes and clothes and laid down on the bed and was soon asleep. Dog checked the kitchen several times and then came in and laid down with him.

The next morning Dwight got up around ten and sat on the back porch with Dog, drinking coffee and smoking. He replayed the scene at the house with the man and the girl several times, still shocked at what he had done. The little girl kept coming to the front of his thoughts and he finally forced himself to get up and stop thinking about it.

He cleaned the house a little and managed to mow the lawn one handed. Bored now, he got Dog and drove to the movie store. He got four movies and decided he was hungry and went through the House of Asia drive through and ordered a mess of Chinese food. He put the food on the dash so Dog wouldn't spill it all over the place and drove home. He and Dog ate out of the styrofoam plates and watched all four movies in a row. Dwight went to sleep on the couch not long after.

He woke up early Monday morning with snot stuffed tight in both nostrils. What was the fucking deal with allergies, he wondered. If someone had allergies when he was a kid, they were weird. But now everyone was allergic to the air.

He kicked Dog out and made his way to Walgreen's, where he looked up and down the medicine aisle, for something to make him feel better. The aisle was full of cures for everything, but he wasn't sure what he had or what would help. He looked around for an employee, but they seemed to have left for the day. He walked over to the pharmacy and stood in line behind a woman for several minutes, got disgusted, and went back to the drug aisle. There was a smell in the aisle now like someone farted. Dwight saw a tall man with tightly cut and oiled hair down toward the end of the aisle, looking over his giant glasses at something on the shelf. He had his pants pulled up high over his pot

belly, showing his white socks. Dwight paused at the
smell, and at the pants. He didn't trust grown men in
high waters, and he hesitated to breathe in that smell.

The man turned and glanced Dwight's way and
quickly dismissed him. Dwight felt a knot growing in
him and he put his hand to his stomach. Miserably
thinking this was not what was happening, he forced
himself to walk down the aisle. The man kept peering
over the different medicines, reading the back of each
one and mumbling, then putting it back or holding on
to it. He had a couple in both hands and Dwight
noticed he had on an old pair of blue jeans, but they
were clean. The faded outline of his wallet bulged out
of his right pocket and there was a golden chain
clasped to one belt loop that snaked into the front
pocket, which had a little bulge in it, like a watch and
some keys, or a pocket full of change, like two or
three dollars worth. He didn't like grown men who
kept a pocket full of change. The man in the aisle
seemed ominous, like he was the character in The
Twilight Zone who was about to get the weird
started. Dwight walked slowly down the aisle, nearer,
trying not to breathe through his nose. He felt the
knot grow and twist around his organs and grip his
insides, like over Abigail's coffin, like the night at The
Shame, and the pain raced up to his eyes and forced
tears into them. He grabbed his stomach tightly
trying to look casual and kept walking. The man had
a yellow short sleeve shirt with a collar, and even
though it was 85 degrees outside, he had on a white
undershirt. As Dwight walked past him, he breathed
in through his nose and immediately caught the smell
full blast, and he realized with a mounting nauseous
pressure, that it was that smell, here again, all over

this man. Abigail was covered in the smell, but he had not thought about it then. He remembered it now, and he remembered it on the couple in the bar and in the house with the little girl as he bent down to kiss her head, and this man here wore it like cologne. He was bathed in it like some women bathed in perfume. He managed to reach the end of the aisle before he fell to his knees. The man behind him said something out loud and the thought of him coming over and bringing the smell with him was more than he could handle and he puked. The loud retching sound filled the back of the store. The man gasped behind him, and Dwight was pretty sure he then walked off. *Thank god, you coward.* He looked at his insides juiced up and spewed all over the tile floor and grimaced. The smell of vomit covered the other smell and made him feel a little better. A short plump woman in a red vest, rounded the corner then stopped short when she saw the vomit. Dwight gave her a little shrug and started to get up.

"Oh my…!"

He looked down the aisle and the man was gone. He steadied himself, wiped his mouth with the back of his hand, glanced at the woman, and then turned, walking away.

"Sir!" She barked at him emphatically. "Are you okay?"

But what Dwight heard her say was, "Who's gonna clean this shit up?" He kept walking, quicker now. The man wasn't at the front counter; the lady there looked at him questioningly, wanting to know what was happening down the aisle He hadn't stopped to buy anything, so he must have left the store. Dwight hurried out the door and looked left and right and over the parking lot but didn't see him. Then he heard a door close and the motor of a small car start. He looked in that direction to see a shadow in the driver's seat of a clean, pewter Dodge truck. The reverse lights came on, and it started backing up. It was one of those small trucks that cost as much as a full-sized truck but can't do half the work, with a license plate that read HUCKSON 1. Dwight saw the oiled head of thinning hair of the man in the store driving away. He stood there watching him drive off and felt sick. *Now what the fuck am I supposed to do?* The pain was subsiding, and with relief he thought it might go away soon. *I can ignore it. I don't know what he's done, so he stinks. So what? What am I supposed to do?* He thought these things to himself as he was walking toward his truck, and he unlocked it and got in. Then he started it up. He sighed as it rumbled to life. Keeping his eye on the little pewter Dodge truck, he backed up and followed it, the pain gnawing at his belly.

He followed the man down the main street through some stop lights and then into a little strip mall parking lot not far from the Walgreens. Dwight eyed some of the signs of the stores as the pewter truck pulled up close to the front door of one of them and parked. Dwight looked up at the sign over the door and read the word "Daycare". He noticed the sign was done in those crayon letters with some of the letters backward like some challenged six-year-old had written the sign. *A daycare.* Dwight parked in an open spot off to the side, killed his truck and looked at his watch. *Who picks up their kid at 8:30 in the morning?* He sat and waited. *Maybe he picks them up and goes home with them, does his thing, and then brings them back before their parents pick them up. Maybe he doesn't do anything with them*, he thought as he gripped his stomach and remembered the girl in the bathroom. He looked up at the sign again and then said, "Oh what the fuck…" The sign read "HUCK*SONS* AND *DAUGHTERS* Family Daycare". He was Huckson. He owned the daycare.

Dwight pulled out an old but clean spare work shirt from behind his seat and put it on over his slightly stained puke shirt. He put on his cap and made his way to the front door of the daycare. He opened the door to the smell of cleaning supplies and the noise of kids and TV, and also the waft of the smell beating him in the face. It was like there was an open sewer line in the building, and he wondered how anyone could stand it. He looked around. There were small kids spilled about some bean bags and big stuffed animals, watching Barney by the big front window to the left of the door. It was a large open room sectioned off with different colored carpet and a tile walkway curving down the middle and around a corner toward the back like the yellow brick road or something, and to the right was a desk with a slightly open door to a room behind it, but there was no one at the desk, and he saw no sign of the man from the Walgreens. There were no adults present at all. Two of the little kids began to toddle over to him. Dwight became mad. What was to stop him from grabbing one of these kids and leaving? There was a bunch of kids, four or five years old, watching SpongeBob on a TV a little further back with the volume at defcon 4 and no one would hear.

One of them turned and looked at him and then hollered out, "Misses Huckson! There's someone heeerrrrree!" Still no one showed. The little girl who'd done the hollering got up and started for the open door behind the desk, "Misses Huckson…!" One of the older group, a boy clutching a chocolate pudding cup in one hand with pudding on his shirt and fingers and no spoon in sight, approached Dwight.

"What's your little boy's name?" He said to Dwight, and after giving him a nanosecond to answer asked him again, "What's your little boy's name? My name's Braden." He put a finger in the pudding cup.

Dwight heard a shuffle in the closed room and presently "Misses Huckson" appeared. She was disheveled and hurried looking with an odd mass of poofy red hair on her head and giant glasses that sat crooked on her face, sort of completing the look.

"Can I help you?" She said, letting him know she did not want to help him, and she did not want to be bothered by him. He studied her for a moment too long before answering, and a cloud came over her face as she glanced at the cast on his hand and in a mean tone she said, "Is there something you need?"

He hated her instantly. "I heard you have a great daycare here, and I'd like to see about getting my son in. Do you have an application I can take home?"

"We're all full, and I don't think I have any applications." She said, making no move to look for any applications.

He heard a man's high nasty laughter filter in from the back of the building and around the corner and his stomach knotted up. "I'll look around a moment while you look for that application," he said, walking straight to the back. She huffed loudly but did not stop him. He passed the little group watching Spongebob and turned the corner. There was an open door immediately to his left. He looked in and saw another TV, showing some Japanimation cartoon where the characters yell everything they say but it was turned down low. There were two kids about six years old with their faces nearly attached to the screen, and in two corners of the room stood a boy sitting with his back to the corner, one looking upset and the other looking off into space. In the third corner, farthest from the door, the man with his high waters and his well combed plastered down hair was sitting in a plastic orange chair and was just pulling a little boy onto his lap. He had his hands and arms draped around the boy like a spider. The little boy squirmed as he was pulled up and reached out his hands grabbing at the air futilely. His little face was scrunched up, and he wriggled valiantly but he was pulled up anyway.

Dwight entered the room, walking right up to him. He looked up at Dwight, startled, his eyes wide behind his eighties glasses. He regained his composure quickly and looked at Dwight with contempt, then at his cast and his clothes. He started to say something like 'what's going on?' or "what's your problem?' but Dwight leaned into him and spoke in a quiet voice so the other kids couldn't hear.

"Shut your fuckin' mouth. I *know* what you're doing." He locked eyes with him as he spoke, and he reached down slowly and grabbed the boy's hand, who was staring up at him. The stench of the smell was shimmering up in his face like heat waves. He pulled him gently out of his lap and let him go in the direction of the TV, and as he expected, the man sat

55

there and made no effort to stop him. Dwight hovered over him now, trying not to breathe through his nose, the stench wafting everywhere.

"How many kids…" He didn't really know what to say. He let Abby slip into his mind and the rage swelled up in him. In the delay, the man started to huff up out of the chair and demand what he was doing here, but Dwight put a finger in his face and held him in place. The memory of what had been done to his daughter played grotesquely in his mind. He breathed heavily into his face, his words thick and heavy. "How many kids have you put your nasty fucking hands in their pants? How many of them have had to touch you? Do you fuck them?"

He said nothing, his eyes wide, but he pressed back in the chair as far as he could get and looked quickly to the door, like a cat in a corner. Dwight leaned in further, putting his hands on the arms of the chair, almost mounting him. The smell was burning his eyes.

"I *know*. I was *told*. Touch another one. Put your nasty fucking hands on one more of them, I will kill you…"

The man licked his quivering lips, nervous to the point of bolting, his eyes darting from Dwight to the door and back to Dwight. Dwight wanted to hit him so badly. The only thing that stopped him from doing it right here was the children. "You won't go to jail," he said softly. The stench was making it hard to breathe, and he knew he had to leave. He backed up a step and looked around at the children, most of whom were not even paying attention to them. "Not one more, motherfucker," he spit out at him. He turned and walked quickly out the door, leaving him still in the seat, nearly running over Mrs. Huckson as he turned down the hall.

"Oh!" she flustered. He brushed past her. He didn't know what she said after that as he tuned her out and focused on the front door which seemed to be an amazing distance away. His head was throbbing, and it felt helicopters whomping in his ears. He pictured the both of them running after him, her yelling that he had to get out and him saying to call the police, and Dwight beating them both all over the place with the kids watching. He waded through children and toys and pushed his way out the door. He turned right out the door and walked quickly down the strip mall and found a book store and went in. He was shaking and sweating, and he hid himself in the back of the store grabbing a book. He felt tears in his eyes, and his nose was clogged with snot. He tried to breathe slowly as he hid his face in the book, finally calming down when the nausea and pain began to abate. Dwight walked slowly around the bookstore for a long time, avoiding the front windows. He stayed in the dog section for awhile and found a book that said something about boxers. He finally went to the counter and bought it. Before he went outside, Dwight quickly took off his outer shirt and his cap. He scanned the parking lot as he left, looking up and down the row of stores. He slunk the long way around back to his truck. The pewter dodge was gone. A shiver went up his back as he saw the empty spot. *Where did he go, to the police?*

He drove home in a daze, a hollow feeling inside him. He went in the house and let Dog in from the back. Dog bristled immediately and sniffed him all over, snorting and sneezing as he went.

Dwight went over to the couch and sat down numbly, letting himself be inspected. Dog climbed on the couch with him when he was done, looking at him, wondering if they were going to do something. Eventually he lay his head down and slept, as Dwight was already doing.

Almost an hour later the phone rang loudly in his sleep. His mind wandered around consciousness for a bit and then it snapped into place. He picked up the phone and looked at it. It was 10:14 am. He was thirty minutes late. He saw who the missed call was from and listened to the voicemail.

"Yeah Dwight, this is Gerald, I understood you to say you'd be back Monday, uh today, and we didn't schedule to cover your absence, so…if I misunderstood ya, um, just let me know so I can schedule it. Okay, just give me a call when you can. Thanks. See ya."

He sat up on the couch and put his head in his hands. "Oh fuckin' shit…what the fuck am I doing? Am I the goddamn child molester police? Huh? …just drive around looking for mutherfuck…perverts. Why? Why do they do that?" Dog, who'd been listening, began to lick his hands and his ears, anywhere he could get in. Dwight moved his hands and endured the warm and wet onslaught on his face for a few seconds. He hugged him tightly and Dog's nub worked furiously back and forth. "Ok, ok Dog, get the fuck off," he said softly. "C'mon. Get your dumb ass outside. I gotta go to work."

He put in the remaining hours of the day mopping floors and cleaning bathrooms, thankful for the mind-numbing, time-killing, life-sucking thing that was this job. He got a little dressing down from Gerald when he got there, and Dwight felt like telling him it wasn't fucking worth it. But he let Gerald puff his chest out until he felt right about it. He worked with a balled up knot crammed in his gut all day. Occasionally it churned and re-adjusted itself to let him know it was still there. He also thought it was letting him know that the guy was still there at the daycare, still pulling children onto his lap. His anger boiled as he worked, and he purposely used his broken hand more than he had to, to remind him that it was broken, to remind him that he had broken it on a man's mouth as he crushed his teeth in, and to remind him why.

Gerald left at five and Dwight lied to Avaristo and told him he had made arrangements with Gerald to leave early to pick up some medicine for his hand. Avaristo didn't have much to do with Dwight or anyone else, and he gave an I-don't-give-a-shit nod.

He thought the daycare would probably be open until 6 p.m. or so to let people pick their kids up after work but he sped through town, cursing and giving old ladies the stink eye, afraid they would be closed when he got there. He arrived in the parking lot in front of the daycare about 5:20, and saw parents hurrying in and out, dragging kids along with them. He wondered if any of them ever noticed a change in their child. Maybe they had a sullen, sad look on their sweet little faces, or maybe they tore shit up when they got home, refused to do what they were told, or pissed the bed. He hunched down in his truck and waited, watching them go, wanting to scream at them. He didn't see the pewter truck but he hadn't expected to. He let his wife do all the work, and he just got the kids. He was at home right now, watching TV or polishing his bowling ball or playing with himself.

Mrs. Huckson finally made her way through the door about 6:08 with her wild red hair billowing in the breeze and she turned to lock the door. She got into a little, white, four-door foreign car and sped off. Dwight followed.

Like he thought, they lived very close, only about six blocks away. She parked on the street. The pewter dodge was up in the lone spot in the driveway. *Of course it would be.*

Dwight drove on past. Earlier, he noticed on the door of the daycare that it opened at 6:45am. He would be back here at 6:30am. He headed to The Shame.

He sat down in his spot at The Shame and had his drinks without saying much to anybody. He remembered Belly's behavior with his daughter, but neither one talked about it, and a few hours later Dwight paid up and left. He got some sliders for himself and Dog on the way home. They ate and he set his alarm and fell right to sleep with Dog watching and wondering.

The next morning the fat, little daycare worker, who Dwight guessed probably had an idea what her husband was doing to her little charges but didn't worry too much about it, waddled her way out of the house at 6:30a.m.and after locking the door behind her, got in her car and drove quickly down the street. Dwight was parked halfway down the block and he got out and walked up to the house after she left. He had found his old mid-eighties Rambo hunting knife and had it with him, hanging out of his back pocket. *Knock or just try to open the door? No fingerprints. Fuck it.*

He knocked loudly on the door. After a couple seconds he put his thumb over the eyehole and knocked rapidly again. Maybe he'll think it's her, he thought.

"Just wait a minute Audra." He heard him say tersely through the door. He heard the dead bolt slide back and saw the knob turn. As the door opened Dwight pushed the door open and stepped into the house and locked eyes with him.

"*Now you can't…!*" he started to say, backing up in angry surprise. Dwight smelled the smell here, but not much, it was just on him. He didn't do it here. Dwight suddenly knew he would help out at the daycare when he wanted some. He would give his wife a break and let her go buy groceries or get her wild hair done. Then he would take one of them in a back room of the daycare and get his feel on. Dwight saw the sweat on his pasty cheeks and the fresh oil on his nasty slicked back hair, saw the haughtiness and fear in his dull brown eyes through his big coaster sized glasses. He imagined a little boy lured into the back room of the daycare where they weren't allowed to go, with the promise of candy, a reward for being good. Then the door would shut and he would be alone in the room with Mr. Huckson and Mr. Huckson would begin. Then the wrongness of what Mr. Huckson was doing to him, making him do, would settle in on him. The boy's whole idea of what adults were supposed to do, the right and wrong, was now all wrong. Not understanding, not nearly old enough to understand what was happening and why it was happening to him, but unable to stop it, and then Dwight stepped closer pulling the knife out from behind his back and lunged into him, ramming it quickly in and out of his belly.

He let out a loud grunt, his eyes huge and bulged out were staring down at the knife, then quickly pressed his hands against his shirt, fear and confusion all over his face. He took a step back and took his hands away and looked down at them, and then at this shirt. He moaned a little and quickly put his hands back over the wound. He stumbled back and half bent over. *What is happening?* Dwight could see the question on his face as he brought his hands away from his stomach to check again, and they both stared at the blood on his hands. Dwight stepped up quickly and rammed him again with the knife, in and out, and he began to fall to the floor and Dwight went down with him and stabbed him again and again. He pulled away from Dwight and balled up on the floor, moaning and coughing. Dwight stood up, looking down, trying to decide if it was enough. He just wanted him to be dead. He listened to the noises he made, anguished gasps and grunts and raspy breathing, but he did not seem to be slowing. Dwight knelt down behind him and looked at where he thought his kidney would be. He braced himself and jabbed the knife in his back. The man arched his back wildly and yelled out, his legs shooting straight out. He reached slowly to his back with his right hand, like he didn't really want to but couldn't stop. Dwight jerked the knife out and he gasped a crying sound, his hand and arm frozen in mid air for a moment. He rolled slowly over on his back and rested one hand gently on his abdomen the other laid down by his side, his eyes staring at the ceiling.

Dwight stood up. The man's breathing was fast, but Dwight could see it slowing. He saw the ever-reddening yellow shirt still tucked in neatly. He watched him as his body began to relax and he lay peacefully on the floor. After a minute, Dwight kicked him in the side. He barely flinched.

Dwight refused to look any more, moving his eyes away to look around the home. It was full of knickknacks and fake flowers and fake plants. Orange and green colors dominated the house. He stepped into the brightly lit kitchen. *There must be ten lights on in here.* He paused, leaning against the door frame, closing his eyes and listening to his own breathing. After a moment, he opened his eyes and saw an orange hand towel hanging on a hook on a cabinet and he grabbed it, wrapping the knife with it then stuffing it in his pants with his shirt hanging over it. He walked back through the living room, stopping to glance at the body on the floor for several seconds. No movement. He opened the door using his shirt and pulled it closed behind him, walking casually but quickly to his truck, and drove home.

Once home, Dwight went straight to the garage and locked himself in. He got out the grinder and put the blade in the vice and went to work on it. The whine of the grinder reverberated loudly in the garage and he wondered if any of his neighbors could hear it. He forced the wheel onto one spot on the blade, determined to saw it in two, and the sparks flew off in a streaming shower over the bench and onto the floor. His broken hand began to hurt. Sweat stuck his shirt to his back and collected in his eyebrows, threatening to cascade into his eyes, and after several minutes he stopped grinding. The knife was mutilated but not beyond incrimination. As he was looking it over, he heard Dog whine in the backyard. He put the grinder down and walked over to the back door of the garage and let him in. Dog stood in the garage door and sniffed Dwight up and down for several intense seconds, the hackles standing up on his back, before snorting, and then he came on in to inspect the garage. Dwight felt his calm returning while Dog checked him out. He was shaking, but he felt all juiced up. The heat of the garage felt good and the air smelled burned and metallic. He leaned against the work bench holding the knife and breathed in deeply, closing his eyes.

He felt Dog's nose against his hand and he looked down at him. "Well what the fucka.m.I gonna do with the knife, Dog?" Dog eyed him seriously. *Wrap it in plastic and throw it away. Nobody's gonna go through your trash.* He didn't think the dog had come up with this idea, but it sounded good. He took the knife out of the vise and wrapped it in a small garbage bag and shoved it in a hamburger helper box he had in the trash can. Then he shoved the box down into the trash and put the lid back on. He looked at it for several seconds, then let Dog in the house and went to take a shower and get ready for work.

CHAPTER 6

Later that day, Dwight plodded numbly through his duties. The reality of what he had done made him tired. It was like he was two different things. One was an automated body completing the chores required to not get fired. The other was the mind of a smooth metal pinball bouncing back and forth, banging into the same few thoughts in random order. He had killed two people, and the second one he had actually tracked down, stormed into his home and knifed to death. But he felt good! Sort of. There was no wrenching pain in his stomach. He felt okay, tired but okay. He was absolutely sure about the first one, and he felt pretty good about the second one. Dwight knew what he had been doing at that daycare. *Sick fucker.* He shivered inside, remembering the smell and the nausea. He had *reeked* of it, like cologne. Dwight wondered if that meant he'd done a lot of it. Then he straightened up. Is that what the smell was? Was it like, a meter or something? Going off when molesters where near?

He wondered about the daycare. It didn't look new. All the stuff was used and worn. He got angry thinking how long they'd probably been in business, about how many kids he'd abused. He rammed the mop into the corners of the bathroom and into the toilets thinking of his smug high and mighty face, his perfectly combed thinning greased hair. Dwight thought of him with the knife first in his gut, backing up from the door as he entered the house and entered the knife into him. He was probably thinking *this is unexpected*, and then Dwight bowled over, suddenly laughing. He dropped the mop and got down to his knees in the stall and he laughed and laughed, his head leaned over nearly touching the toilet. Tears came from his eyes as the laughing began to change into crying before he could stop it. He cried loudly and freely, alone in an office building after hours, alone on the third floor men's bathroom. He bawled and thought of Abby and the ache of losing her filled his bones and his heart, and he cried for her. His throat swelled up. Before he could stop himself, he imagined his daughter alone with the man, the man who got her to jump the fence and come inside to see his puppy when she knew she shouldn't, and her father was nowhere to tell her no, Honey. He thought of her alone with the man who took her to another house, when she told him she didn't want to go, told him that she couldn't go, but he would not stop, and he became mean at the other house, and then he started in on her. WHERE WAS HER DADDY? Dwight's mind threatened to crack as his heart hammered away in his chest. He forced himself to stop it and shut his mind's eye off. *No more, I can't take anymore!*

He screamed into the bathroom, "I GOT TWO OF THEM ABBY! I GOT TWO OF THEM!" He huffed and hit the stall with his fist. *"They* won't do it anymore. They're done," he said softly, folding against the toilet. After a few moments, he rose to his feet, picking up the mop, and left the rest of the bathroom undone.

After work he drove straight for The Shame and sat down slowly just as Belly came in from the back.

He frowned and looked at the clock. "You're early bud." He started making up a drink for him. He set it down on the bar, and Dwight put it back down empty a few moments later.

Belly stared at him and then the glass for a second before saying, "I'm gonna get you a bigger glass." He smiled at him, and Dwight felt his heartbeat slow down, his mind suddenly empty again. Belly made him another drink and said, "Are you good for a minute or do I need to piss in a glass?"

Dwight got out a cigarette and lit it. "I don't know," he said, still a little edgy. "That depends on two things. How much do you normally piss? A glass might not hold it all, and then you'd have to pinch it off and you'd be dripping everywhere and that'd be gross. You might need a pitcher. Secondly, how long is your minute? I mean, if I'm thinkin' sixty seconds and you go play with your ding-dong in the bathroom for five minutes, there'll be a problem. I could die."

Belly had begun to walk off before Dwight finished. "Well, that's a chance I'm willin' to take."

Dwight continued a little louder, "You don't take very good care of the only person sad enough to come in here every day, you know. You're really not a very good bartender. Drunks are special, and I need more attention than these run-of-the-mill "let's go have a couple a drinks" people. I mean, shit, really. Who goes out and has a couple of drinks? I have a couple of drinks to *think* about going out and drinking. Jesus."

Belly came back and made Dwight a third drink and made himself one too.

He held up the drink he made for himself and said, "This is on your tab."

Dwight looked at the the new drink sitting on the bar Belly had made for him like it wasn't his. "Did you wash your hands?"

"Shut the fuck up. I'd say choke on it but I don't want the cops here. Looks bad."

"You look bad." Dwight looked around the empty bar dramatically and said, "We closed today?"

Belly said, "Shit, we're closed everyday. I don't know why I keep unlocking the door."

Dwight smoked his cigarette, and they sat silent for a few moments. Dwight said, "Do you make any money with this place? I mean, you're not going broke are you?"

Belly leaned against the bar finishing his drink. "Not really. I made some good money in the beginning. Man this place was hot, and I don't know why. I don't know why it's so slow now. The economy, I guess. The weekends are keeping me open but I might as well close Sunday through Wednesday. I've thought about it."

Dwight eyed him through a cloud of smoke. "You fuckin' bastard." Belly smiled at him. Dwight said, "Can you make me a key? I'll come in here by myself. I might like that better."

Belly said, "Shit no. By the time I got here on Thursday there'd be no vodka left. You'd probably sleep on the pool table."

"I'll bring a cot."

He spent the rest of the week feeling better than he had in a long time. He got off work and spent the evenings with Belly until 10 p.m. or so, made a pit stop at White Castle or Taco Bell and then he and Dog ate like kings. He slept until about six a.m.when Dog wanted out, then he slumbered until the alarm went off at 9 a.m. On Saturday morning, Dwight took Dog to the dog park and let him run himself around. Dog was a running fool. He smelled all the way around every tree and every piece of dog climbing thing there was, occasionally leaving a message or two. Dwight thought that's what they might be, dog post-it notes, or ad columns. 'Single long-haired dog likes riding in cars and eating cat food, seeking companion for fun and frolic, with some heavy butt sniffing later'.

He looked over at the little playground across the way from the dog park and saw some kids bouncing around all over the equipment. He looked around for parents and found a few sitting on benches nearby, looking at their phones. Don't do it, he thought. Don't look away.

He would like to sit on one of the benches and watch the kids play, but he didn't. He thought the moms would be worried about Dog, and he didn't want to look like a pervert. So he sat down on a bench in the dog park and stared off into space while

Dog ran around leaving and checking messages. They stayed for about an hour and then left.

On the way home from the park, Dwight stopped in gas station to get a soda and as he stood in line he saw the newspaper headlines. On the front page was the story of a man who'd been murdered in his home, brutally stabbed six times with a large knife. Dwight was mesmerized. He had killed that man. He knew without reading the story it was his guy. He bought the paper and drove home.

The story read like one of those new detective shows that glorify the criminal by graphically describing every detail known about the crime. And what details they didn't have, they gleefully ascribed the many possibilities. Dwight was horrified, sickened, and also a little embarrassed. He felt like calling the paper and telling them what they'd gotten right and wrong. *Hi, that guy you've got splayed out on your front page there, yeah that was me, and here's what really happened.* On the front page though? Why did murder have to be on the front page? It was news, for sure, but why was it always the first thing they told you? *Hey look it, a violent thing happened today and here's how many people died and here's all their names. It was a fucking great day, buy this paper.*

They had no leads in the case and were looking for help from the public. They gave details about the victim, saying he had retired from the post office, and he and his wife had operated their daycare for the past fifteen years, and some other boring crap. Fifteen years, thought Dwight. He wondered when he began with kids. Was it before the daycare, maybe his own kids, or some nephews? He imagined him encouraging his wife to open the daycare, telling her she was great with kids and blah blah blah. Dwight felt vindicated somehow by the article even though it hadn't said anything negative about Huckson. He guessed he'd been after kids for years, probably decades, and he wished he'd run him through a few more times.

He found himself at The Shame around 1pm, his drink on the bar was watered down with melted ice by the time he got there. He had quite a good time at The Shame for most of the day and into the night. During the afternoon, he mentioned the lady Belly had talked with at the table the other day. Belly didn't seem to mind talking about it, and confirmed what Dwight thought; it was his daughter, and she was involved with a total loser whose job in life was to make her miserable and he was good at it. He and Belly discussed the situation for a while. It was the most they'd ever talked and Dwight felt good about talking with him. They weren't really friends yet, but it was a start. Friendship with guys took time, it was a slow thing sometimes, like cooking brisket. If you rushed it, you burned the edges and the inside didn't cook. Men didn't like to say, "Hey you wanna be friends?". It developed unspoken. Guys knew they were friends by how they treated each other; with respect and actually caring about what you said. You didn't want to help too much though. It said you thought he couldn't do it by himself. It was just being around and there to help if he asked. Or picking him up when he got knocked down, and then acting like it was no big deal.

Belly said her ex-boyfriend might have pushed her around some but nothing too serious, and Belly was close to getting her to accept how he really was, and how he was gonna stay. She had one kid from a previous marriage, but no kids with the current loser, which was easier. He and Dwight talked about it for awhile and decided Belly had her just about out of the relationship, but Dwight offered to kill him for fifty bucks anyway.

He didn't drink at his usual pace tonight. The desperate need to *numb* wasn't so persistent, but he still probably drank more alcohol than anyone in there. He sat at the bar and watched people mix the liquor into their lives, and thought it must be a great thing to own a bar. This was medicine, and Belly was the doctor. They came in there because they needed something else, something their families, their friends, their jobs and their hobbies couldn't provide. They wanted to get a little drunk and get brave so they could feel better about themselves and have the courage and confidence to be the person they thought they were. A little bit of alcohol pulled the person they wanted to be out from behind the door and let him dance. A lot of alcohol would bring that person's stupid out, who was hiding behind the basement door, and it would make a right ass of everything. Dwight let his stupid out on Saturdays sometimes. He laughed a little to himself and he thought, If you didn't let the stupid out once in a while it might just bust out on its own and never get back behind the door.

He watched a cowboy and his girl walk in. He liked the way they looked and he checked on them every now and then. They were having a good time for a while, but then what seemed like old arguments came out and pretty soon he noticed they weren't talking. There was love there, Dwight could plainly see, but they had something gnawing at them, like a thorn they couldn't find. He felt sorry for them, as neither one seemed the bad guy. Dwight tried to figure out what the problem was. Cheating? That was the problem most of the time. He didn't understand why no one today could remain faithful. He would have liked to get with more than half the women he saw when he was married, but he never did and he never even tried. Some people didn't take their vows too seriously. But there wasn't that look to their mood. It was deep, but they were still close to each other and they still touched occasionally with neither pulling away. Money? They were smartly dressed but not overdone, and she wasn't laid out with diamonds. She had a nice ring, but that spoke to Dwight of love, not show. She had no other ring on. Dwight thought about that a moment as he watched her. She had long blond hair that hung straight down her shoulders, not much makeup on and her yellow cowgirl shirt was undone only two buttons. She had little gold hoops in her ears and a little gold chain with a ring on it. A promise ring Dwight thought. She had two rings on, one on her finger and one around her neck.

What could their problem be? He watched them and it seemed serious, both of them seemed pretty upset. *Work it out,* he found himself thinking. He was a tall, good looking cowboy with a straw Stetson on his head. Dwight made a face at the hat. He wondered where the good manners of taking your hat off indoors went. Cowboys were supposed to be well mannered, *yes ma'am*, and all that. He looked around at all the baseball caps on heads and sighed. Well this was a bar, did that rule apply in bars?

Maybe not. Was that rule even a thing anymore? Probably not. He thought all these idiots would still have their hats on in a restaurant or in their momma's house.

The cowboy wasn't making eyes at anybody and wasn't swinging his swagger around either. Dwight wanted to help them. He wanted to send them a drink, but that would be weird. The cowboy looked up and caught Dwight looking. He turned back to his girl and made a few comments and they decided to take their problem elsewhere. He didn't call for his tab, he just caught Joni's eye and set some money down on the bar. Classy, thought Dwight. He was glad they left. He imagined a serious talk in the car, but at least they were going home together. And he realized he was a bit drunk, and he wondered seriously for the first time since he'd gotten divorced, if he might take someone home.

He scanned the people sitting around the bar and found it populated with four women and about ten men. Two of the women were obviously taken but Dwight couldn't understand why as he looked at them. *Scraggly.* The other two were sitting next to each other, sandwiched in by hovering men. They looked to be working though, and Dwight didn't think either girl was worth the trouble. *Why are bar flies ugly?* His eye fell on Joni as she leaned against the bar chatting with Tom and his old beat up wife. Man, Tom's wife was rough, but Tom was a serious rummy, and they were tied together for what was left of their lives. Joni had a nice shape if somewhat short and a little dumpy. She was bar tired, though, and she'd be here until she got too old. He looked around for Karen and found her rump, as she was bent over fiddling with something under the sink.

"Belly!" she yelled. "Belly this fucking sink ain't draining again." As she straightened up, she kicked the pipes underneath. Dwight smiled. Karen was lively for sure, and she didn't do anything unless it was loud. She was pretty cute too, though she was a little younger than he was. She wasn't knockout cute though, but he thought her attitude was all balls. She had a mouth that made the old timers wince. Old Tom loved her. She had an Indian ritual tattoo on her lower belly that kinda looked like a chicken and he was always trying to get her to show him the chicken. It was a joke with the regulars. Karen noticed Dwight looking at her and she walked up to him. "You doin' alright Dwight? Can I get you another drink?" She laughed a friendly little laugh.

"I'm much better now," he said.

"Why? Cuz I'm standing next to you?" She gave the little laugh again.

Yes, he thought, but did not say. It was wrong with Karen, to bar flirt with her like you were serious.

"You want another drink?" she asked again. She looked at his nearly full drink. For some unspoken reason Joni was in charge of refilling his drinks. "No, you're okay. You want a water? Are you hungry? You want some chips or something? I think we got some cut up cheese left, you want some? Huh?" She looked at him expectantly waiting for something to jump on.

"Well, which one a those questions do you want me to answer? If you need me to answer more than one of 'em," he said slowly, "I'm gonna need you to write them down, and then I'll need a pencil and some paper." The bar around him laughed, and she let out her patented Karen laugh and Dwight realized he liked her. She was solid. She had sand, as the old timers would say, and she had plenty of it. She was full blast and top down. He watched her walk away. She hadn't given him anything she'd suggested. His smart ass had been too smart.

He melted slowly into his vodka and coke as the evening receded and he was not unhappy. The night drug on, and he wanted to take Karen home. He would not ask her, though, he would not make a move on her. He knew, somehow, that she would be offended if he hit on her now, after hours of drinking and sitting there doing nothing. So, he sat contentedly and watched her without staring. She was a diamond gone unnoticed. You wouldn't want to pick her up and dust her off though; she would lose some of her charm. She was dusty brilliant. And Dwight was satisfied he had noticed.

It was towards closing time, and he had hung on longer than he ever had, mostly mooning over Karen, but now he was tired and ready to go. He fished out five twenties and set them under his glass. He said goodbye to Joni and returned a nod from Belly. He saw Karen was engaged at the other end of the bar, and he was on his way to the door when he heard someone say, "…fucking bitch!" in her proximity. He pulled up short and watched as a fat young man stood up in front of Karen. Dwight's pissed-off meter starting dinging.

"Well she has; she's been a fucking bitch all night," he said to his little girlfriend.

"Yeah, well, you ain't the first buddy," Karen said loudly.

Dwight was in front of him in two steps and swaying just slightly. "Did you," and he stuck his finger in his chest, "call her," and he pointed to Karen without looking at her, "a *fucking bitch*?" The bar around them went quiet. To Dwight's surprise he stood his ground, and Dwight wondered if he was drunk or just confident, but then he caught the little girlfriend's very concerned look.

"Yes I did. She is," and he began to punctuate every word, "*A. Fucking. Bitch!*"

Dwight knew where he was going to hit him before he got the last word out. His left hand smashed into the left side of his mouth just as he finished. It had the effect he thought it would. The young man's head snapped back and he began to tip over, his arms outstretched and waving. Dwight hoped he would keep right on going over, as there was nothing behind him to break his fall. A shot to the mouth and a long trip down to the floor might be enough. Everyone watched as he tumbled over backward and he fell to the floor in a loud display. Some people laughed. It was an awkward fall, and Dwight suppressed a laugh. He looked over at the girlfriend and winked. Then Belly was there pushing Dwight roughly toward the door. He said quickly to Dwight, "Hurry up and get out, man, he'll call the police," and then loudly he said "Get out you fuckin' drunk! And don't come back!"

Dwight sauntered out of the bar and through the parking lot to his truck feeling pretty good. He hadn't been able to take her home, but he had sure defended her honor! He thought about her all the way home, sometimes with a big grin on his face, and as he walked to the front door of his house still smiling and heard Dog's excited short bark in the backyard, he realized he hadn't even stopped for late night groceries. Though he was still pretty drunk, he let dog out the front door, who then bounced all over the yard, and they got in the truck and headed out, two bachelors on the loose looking to fill their bellies.

CHAPTER 7

A few days later, Dwight was at work bagging the trash in the main lobby, when he heard the elevator doors ding open. He stopped as he bent over the bag to tie it up when he felt a knot crawl into his stomach. He jerked his head up and looked around. There was no one immediately in sight but the elevator was around the large plant pyramid and water fountain in the center of the lobby, and he was not in a position to see if someone had gotten on or off the elevator. He walked quickly around the fountain and saw the door of the elevator as it closed, heading up and no one around. He looked at the front door of the building and saw the glass door as it closed. Did he get off the elevator and leave the building, and then someone called the elevator back up, or did he come in the building and take the elevator up himself? Dwight walked over to the elevator door and there it was, the smell, lingering and disgusting. He walked to the front door and breathed in, trying not to gag. It was stronger here and his gut rumbled around and sent little cramps everywhere.

God, he thought, *is this thing alive in me?* He pushed his way out the door and looked left and right, seeing no one. Then he heard a car start in the parking lot off to the left of the building. He walked around and saw a little yellow Ford Festiva coming out of the lot. He stared openly at the driver as he went by. The guy looked right and then left as he started to leave, and as he looked left he saw Dwight staring at him. He was a large man, hunched over the little steering wheel. He had a white t-shirt with some saying on it, like one you could buy at Walmart. Their eyes met and Dwight hunched over in pain. He looked up as the Festiva took a right out of the parking lot and headed quickly down the street. Dwight straightened up, unsure what to do. His gut churned as if it was disgusted with him.

"Well, what the fuck am I supposed to do? Follow him?," Dwight said aloud, exasperated. He still had his uniform on, the trash was still all piled up and his cleaning supplies were still scattered over three floors. It was only 4:30 and he still had two hours to work. *Fuck it.* He'd take a quick break. He got in his truck; already the car was out of sight, but it was a yellow Festiva, he might find it.

He sped out of the parking lot and took a right. He kept straight, looking quickly down each side street as he passed, running two yellow lights. After a few blocks, he began to think he'd lost him. As he approached another yellow light on a main intersecting street, he quickly decided to turn left, sliding through what was now red light. He searched ahead as far as he could see and got excited when he saw a little yellow spot in the traffic five or six blocks up, and he sped up, weaving through cars. Then he

heard a loud Whoop! Whoop! and saw a police car
slip in behind him, with it's lights all ablaze. He
gripped the wheel tightly with his good hand and let
off the gas. He looked ahead and watched as the
yellow spot disappeared. He made no attempt to pull
over in a safe place as he might have normally. He
was suddenly furious and he jerked his truck over
immediately to the curb, still well in the lane of traffic
and came to an abrupt stop. He clutched angrily at
his stomach as it knotted in protest.

　　After a few minutes sitting in his car, the
policeman got out purposefully and walked up to
Dwight's truck. Dwight watched him and saw he had
that slow, *I'm a badass* cop walk. Dwight never rolled
down his window and as the officer approached, he
just looked at him. He rapped his knuckles on the
window sharply. Dwight rolled it about two-thirds
down and stared into the reflective *I'm a bad ass* cop
glasses, and he felt his stomach do flip-flops in an all
out riot but he managed a hostile, "Yeah?"

　　The nauseating smell, that smell, wafted, no
poured into the truck and hit Dwight with the force of
a fist. The officer was saying something, but Dwight
could not focus, as he could not breathe, and he
doubled over in the seat and tried to lean away from
the window, and his left hand reached vainly for the
button to roll it up.

　　"Whoa! Whoa, buddy! You okay there?" He
eyed Dwight seriously.

　　Dwight did not understand what was
happening, but he could barely move and he could
not breathe. The man in the Festiva was long gone
and the smell, the pain, should have left with him. It
was like getting punched in the gut, just below your

sternum where you absolutely could not breathe for several seconds.

The officer was saying something and trying to open the door. He tried to straighten up, he reached out for something and felt the strong hand of the officer, pulling him upright, still jabbering with concern, and Dwight suddenly felt the urge, the *need* to kill him, to run him through with something, and he realized the pain, and *this* smell, was coming from him. The officer had his own smell.

Dwight made it straightway up and looked over at him, feeling the acute rumble in his stomach. Then he puked with intense pain, and also with determined intent, all over the officer's pants.

The officer jumped back with a yell, almost into traffic. Dwight righted up again and gave him a weak, loony smile.

"…the fuck man!"

Dwight laughed inside. "I got the flu, man, sorry. I was tryin' to make the clinic." He could think of nothing else to say except, "If you could gimme the ticket, I think, I can make it okay. To the clinic."

The officer looked down disgustedly at his pants. "Holy shit. Hoolleee shit. You think you can make the clinic, huh? That's fucking awesome. Well you just go goddamn right ahead. Mother fuck!"

"Thank you, Officer," he said weakly, eyeing the tag on his chest, J.L. Lopez. "Thanks."

He put it in drive without waiting any further, and left. He took a couple of turns to get away from the officer and stopped into a small gas station. He got the bathroom key and made his way to the bathroom shaking. He got inside and bolted the door

shut behind him, sliding down to the floor with his
back to the door and put his head against his knees
and put his head in his hands. *What the fuck? WHAT
THE FUCK? A cop! Am I supposed to track him down
and kill him in his front door? I don't even know where the
guy in the Festiva is!*

He sat shaking against his knees for several
minutes until he remembered where he was, and
where he was supposed to be, and he realized with
relief that his stomach no longer hurt. He chastised
himself for being a baby and got up and washed out
his mouth and wiped off his face. He returned the
key and made it back to the office. Avaristo had not
missed him and he hurriedly finished his duties. He
punched out at 6:48 and drove cautiously over to The
Shame.

Belly could tell something was wrong with him,
but he didn't ask. It might come out after a few
drinks if he wanted to talk. If he didn't volunteer it,
Belly would try him later.

Dwight sat in the stillness of his neighborhood
dive bar on Wednesday evening, disgusted with
everything. He looked over the little dump that his
bar was, the smoke hanging around the ceiling like
clouds, brown carpet on the walls, some beer signs on
the walls, and one that only had half the neon
working. Old Tom and his snaggly wife sat on the
rounded end away from Dwight, and rambled on
constantly to each other about the same things he
heard them talk about every time, and they sometimes
tried to pull anybody close by into their discussions,
like the Bermuda Triangle of bar conversations. They
were never successful with Dwight.

Dennis was here tonight, like he was sometimes. He was a former bartender at The Shame. He was in his late fifties, pudging and balding. Dwight didn't know why he was no longer a bartender here, but there was some tension between him and Belly every now and then. Dwight figured it had to do with the quickness Dennis got drunk. Five or six beers, and he was as drunk as he was gonna get, which was pretty drunk, but he'd drink the rest of the night. Dwight counted twenty-two beers and two shots in one night. He usually amused himself watching Dennis's drunken decline, but today he just stared into his own drink, watching the ice melt. After more than an hour being there, Dwight realized there was a fourth person at the bar, Belly's daughter. She sat at the end where the spill-over bar began, and he hadn't even noticed her. She glanced at him as he looked her way, and she gave him a quick smile. He nodded back and wondered what she was doing here. Did she need money from Belly, or was she trolling for a new man? Who was watching her kid, Dwight wondered with some disgust. He saw no reason a young woman needed to be at a bar when she had a kid at home to watch. If she needed a man, there were better places.

He got up heavily and went to the bathroom, stumbling a little down the hall. *Drunk already?* he thought. Went he got back to the bar, Belly was replacing his drink. Dwight made no comment as he sat on the stool. Belly eyed him until Dwight looked up.

"What, old man?"

Belly looked him over and said, "What the fuck's wrong with you?" Dwight's face was tired, lined and drawn, like he hadn't been eating. Belly was gonna mess with him some, but he suddenly felt he might have come on too strong. There was something wrong with Dwight. His skin was weathered and white, like a piece of paper left out and rained on. Belly thought he was in his early forties, but just now he looked older. An unwanted smile came out on Dwight's face, and he quickly put it back. He shook his head as if unsure where to start. "Oh. Nothin'. If you shot me, things might get better." Dwight looked off to the left. "You know, just saying."

"What's a' matter, man?" Belly asked plain and quiet, and he stood waiting. Instead, Dwight lit a cigarette and said, "What's your daughter doing here? She bored?"

Belly smiled and looked over at her. She smiled at them and to Dwight's discomfort, Belly nodded her over. She got up quickly, as if prepared, and Dwight was suddenly horrified to realize this might be a set up. Belly's smile was cut short when he turned back and caught the look on Dwight's face. Dwight tried to change it but it was too late, Belly grabbed some bottles off the bar and smacked them in the trash loudly and Dwight realized he was aggravated. He regretted coming in today.

She sat down in a flush of perfume with some excitement to her, with her large purse, tinkling bracelets, her drink, and a cell phone. She grinned at Dwight and put out her hand. "I'm Audie." Dwight took her hand gently with his left and shook it. It was warm and slightly firm, just right for a woman.

"Dwight. You're Belly's daughter?"

She nodded.

"I'm so sorry," he said. Dwight looked at Belly from the corner of his eye.

"Now," she said with some seriousness, "one thing you don't do is make fun of my daddy while I'm around. Hmmp…," she said rooting around in her purse. "There's a gun in here somewhere." Dwight let go of some of his ill feeling and laughed. She looked up and smiled again. Her smile was infectious. The problems with her loser man must have been pretty well cleared up. *Fuck it. If they wanna set me up, I'll sit here and talk with her for awhile.*

"I got one under here, if you can't find yours," Belly said on his way to the supply room.

"Your dad is a good guy," Dwight said after Belly left.

"Yeah, he is," she said, like a real daddy's girl. "He's helped me out, a lot. This last thing, with Rob, my ex," and she laughed a little like Dwight knew that situation was funny. "I don't know what I would've done if he hadn't helped me." She looked quite sad about it and Dwight could see that if Rob walked in right now and said one right thing, she'd go right back with him. *Stupid girl.*

"This Rob is a real loser, huh?" It had the effect he thought it would.

"Nooo," she turned a frown on him. "He's a good guy; he just has a lot of stress in his life. He's going to school, his ex wife is very needy and she…"

Dwight cut her off, "Where does he work?"

"Well, see, that's another thing. He was working for Layman Brother's construction as a general's assistant…"

"He walked around picking up trash." Dwight cut her off again. She stopped and looked at him, confused.

"The general contractor has two or three lackeys that run around delivering messages, fixing small things on the site, and mostly, they pick up trash and avoid work. They also spy on the other contractors," he said with contempt. He watched her face as she absorbed this new version of Rob's employment. "It takes a real fuck-up to get fired from that. Whatever he told you happened is probably a lie; he got fired. Was he good to you, or just nice at the right times?" She paused long enough and he continued. "You got a little kid," and he paused again and kicked himself for bringing up children. "Don't want just any old jack leg around your child." Belly came back just in time and Dwight said, "Hey Belly, fix us up some poofy shots that your daughter won't object to. Three glasses, too, and hurry it up, old man."

She let the bashing of her ex slide for the moment. "What happened to your hand?" she said, looking at his cast.

He looked at the cast and remembered how he had broken it. "Oh, I didn't like what this guy was doing, so I made him stop doing it." He looked at her sideways a little to see if she would press, and, you know, being a woman, she did.

"Well, did you ask him first?"

"Huh? No. No I didn't," he said. "It wasn't an asking kind of moment."

She smiled at him as Belly set the shots down. "You got a boxer here Daddy."

Belly snorted. "Who, this guy? It's Friday
night fights in here on Saturdays. He picks some
smart ass to spar with and a mike drops down outta
the ceiling and I introduce 'em and we clear the tables
and chairs back and everything. Rope off a little
section and he goes at it, tearin' shit up."

"An I don't get paid for none of it."

They talked like friends for a while. A little later
Dennis left, and Tom herded his wife out. Dwight
imagined him grabbing her by the hair and dragging
her out, with no complaints from her. Then it was
just the three of them, hitting it fairly hard. Belly's
daughter could drink, and Dwight decided she had
probably gotten a good friend or someone to babysit
her kid, and he forgave her for it, and Belly told
stories about Audie as a little girl and a wild teenager,
and he drank and Dwight drank, and they got drunk.

During a lull in the conversation, Belly said,
"You hear about that guy that got stabbed in his own
doorway?" He asked the question expecting they had
already heard about it, the whole city had heard about
this story. There had seemed to be no reason why the
retired postman and owner of a successful daycare
had been attacked and brutally stabbed in his own
living room. None they could find, anyway. Dwight
read that paper the day after, and there had been no
reason known, no leads and no suspects. He had
avoided any news since then.

Audie was shaking her head. Belly said, "Well
two kids at the high school came out yesterday and
said the guy had molested them when they were at his
day care, when they were just little kids." His voice
was low and angry. "Then, two little boys, brothers,
in elementary school, came out and said he'd

88

molested them too, and *now*, they talked with all the kids that's in that daycare and *now* and they think several of them have been abused too. You fuckin' believe that?"

"Oh no!" Audie said. "I hadn't heard that." She stared at the bar in wonder. "How can somebody do that? Why do they wanna do that with little kids?"

Dwight sat still and said nothing, looking off into the dark of the bar. Sweat beaded out all over his skin under his clothes. He felt sticky heat under his arms and suddenly wanted to be somewhere else. He put his cigarette out and lit another one and tried to drink his drink.

"I'd like to meet the guy that killed him," Audie said, "he needs…"

Dwight choked on his drink, he swallowed and coughed at the same time, hacking and spewing coke out his mouth and nose.

Audie patted him roughly on the back. "Are you okay?" She looked at him with worry for a few seconds. Belly handed him a towel and he cleaned himself and the bar up a bit.

"I'm okay. I'm just not used to so much coke in my drink."

"Oh shuddup," Belly said.

"Maybe he needs some milk Daddy," Audie said and she and Belly laughed.

"I can fix you another drink and put a nipple on it?"

"Why don't you fix me a drink and put a lid on it."

"It's no wonder this mother fucker got killed," Belly said as he fixed the drink. "Probably one of those kids' daddy found out what he was doing and killed his ass. Jesus Christ." Belly shook his head. "Fifteen years he'd had that day care open."

They all became silent, feeling the impact of fifteen years of kids being molested. Dwight thought about it silently and then became embolden. He put an end to this monster, this man; people let him have their kids while they went off to work for nine hours, and he had his pick of the litter and he could take off into a private room and do his thing and then put them back in their parents hands with a smile and say "He was pretty good today, but he had some boundary issues, but we had a special talk, and he says he won't do it again, and you owe me $80 dollars a week, you know, for molesting your child while you're at work, okay?"

Audie broke the silence. "Do you have any kids, Dwight?"

Without knowing, she threw one in on his blind side, and Dwight gripped his drink so tightly it might break, as he tried to steady himself. He had guarded himself against the subject earlier, but had since become a little drunk and engrossed in the topic of Will Huckson. She might have smashed her glass in his face for the impact the question had. He freed the glass from his hand and stepped back from the bar, turning away quickly. He took a step and stopped, slowly leaning forward, hunching over like a man cramping.

"Dwight…?" Audie tentatively got up after a queried look to her father. Belly shook his head. He knew Dwight had something, but he didn't know what. It was several seconds later when Audie realized Dwight was crying and she was suddenly

flooded with compassion. She had touched on
something serious and very sensitive. She brushed
past her inhibitions and slipped up in front of him as
he stood frozen. She wrapped her arms around his
waist and pulled him into, doing what only a woman
can, and he fell into her and let go. He bawled like a
child, his face deep into her hair. She supported his
weight as best she could and shooshed him. She felt
his pain rolling out of him, hot and wet on her neck,
and she wondered with some fear what was wrong
with him. He blubbered against her and she realized
he was trying to say something. She rubbed his back
and spoke softly to him and tried to slow him down.
He shuddered and rocked like she had never seen a
grown man do, and she brunted the storm as best she
could, though he was heavy and leaning on her so.
She knew they would soon fall, but then her father
was there with a big arm holding Dwight's shoulder
and leaning against her and he patted him on the
back. Dwight eventually slowed and righted himself a
little, pulling back from Audie reluctantly. He
dropped his hands to his sides, though Audie still held
him by the waist. He looked them both in the eye
through the tears in his own eyes, and then looked at
the floor, and he spoke in a terrible low voice, pulling
it from his guts.

"My little girl, Abigail...was ten. When she was
taken, stolen from me...us. She was playing in the
backyard, while I was in the house, not paying
attention to her, not watching her, and the neighbor
behind us had a friend...sitting their house while they
were on vacation and he...he saw her in the backyard
and somehow he got her into the house, ...and she

went in the house with him…and he took her inside…"

Audie found that she had pulled her hands away from him in horror. He stood alone with his head hung straight down; his hands limp at his side. She watched big tears drip from his eyes and fall to the carpeted floor.

"…he abused her, my god…and then he killed her. HE KILLED MY DAUGHTER!" Dwight exploded his voice into the room and they shrank back from him. "Oh…oh Baby I'm so sorry," he wailed. He sank to his knees and Audie dropped down with him and enveloped him. She crushed him against her with all the might she possessed and unwished this on him. She had never felt for someone so much in her life, and she rocked him and held him. Unsure what to do, Belly kneeled down beside them, putting his arms around them both.

"I'm sorry Dwight," he said. "I'm sorry."

After a minute, Dwight finally raised his head to them and looked at them, and he regained himself a little. He pushed Abigail back into the burnt and wounded place in his heart where he kept her, and he shut the door.

"Okay, okay, get off me," he said quietly.

Belly and Audie got up and went back to the bar and Dwight found his way to the bathroom. He washed his face for several minutes in cold water. He felt okay. *She's gone*, he thought, and he gripped the sink tightly, *but I'm making amends. I am making amends*! And he held on to that because that was all he had.

It was time for him to leave. He left the bathroom and reached to his back pocket for his wallet as he approached the bar, and he caught Belly looking at him. He met his eyes and stopped reaching for his wallet. *Not tonight.* Dwight nodded his head.

He put a hand to Audie's arm touching her slightly. "Thank you, Audie. I'm gonna go…if…"

"Okay Dwight," she said quickly, freeing him of any obligations he thought he might have with her. She had a little piece of paper ready and slipped it into his hand. "Call me, anytime. Anytime. For any reason."

Dwight let her hands go and left the bar.

CHAPTER 8

Dwight scanned the parking lot several times a day at work now, searching for the yellow Festiva. Besides that, there wasn't much he could do about him. That cop, though, he knew his name. He went to the library the next day and found some people using a library computer and he got a book and sat in a chair near them and waited. After a few minutes one of them got up and went to the shelves. He sat down immediately in their chair and searched for J.L. Lopez. He quickly found a probable address and closed out his window and left.

After work on Thursday, Dwight headed to the used car dealership closest to his house. He decided he needed another car if he was going to go around killing people. He found a little white, four-door Kia something or other. He noticed there were plenty of small white, four-door something or others driving around, so he bought this one for fifteen hundred dollars. He drove home in the truck and then walked Dog back up to the dealership and picked up his people-killing car. Dog hopped into the car with a sniff here and there and sat in the front seat waiting for Dwight to get it going. Dwight looked over at him. "You don't care what we do as long as you're in the front seat, do you? You're a car slut, you know that?" He headed out to look for the cop's house.

About ten minutes later, he turned down Maple street slowly and immediately saw a police car parked at the curb. This was him. He rolled casually passed. There was a large white SUV in the driveway and then the cruiser in the street, but no other vehicles belonged at the house. He saw no one outside which was not unusual. There could be twelve people inside and none of them would be in the yard. No one seemed to like to go outside anymore. He drove on past and tried to figure out what to do. If he killed this cop, they would find him. You didn't kill cops and get away with it. They came after you. Dwight wondered who he was molesting. He figured he had kids. All cops seemed to have two or five kids, but most people didn't often molest their own kids. He really didn't want to kill anyone else, no matter how bad they needed it. He didn't know what to do.

He drove the long way home to a pawn shop he knew of a few years ago when he'd been on a bricklaying job in that area and had gone in it a couple times on his lunch break. It was still there. He parked in the front where he could see Dog in the car and went inside. He browsed the DVDs and picked up a couple of stupid ones he'd never seen. He fingered some of the power tools and finally made his way to the gun counter. They had plenty of what anybody needed, from beat up old revolvers to nearly new semi-automatics displayed in nice neat rows under the glass, with the price tags showing. Dwight wondered what he was looking for when his eye cast over into the next case and noticed the knives. He saw two large dull looking hunting knives on the bottom row without much glamor to them and he called the guy over. He looked them over and handled them and haggled with the guy and finally bought them both for twenty bucks. Dwight drove home and put Dog in the backyard. Then he put the Kia in the garage and got out the knives. He sharpened them both with the grinder not caring about ruining the blade, and stashed one in the Kia and then took the other and hopped into his old truck, sticking it under the seat. He noticed the dusty dash of his truck and saw White Castle bag in the floorboard, and was suddenly hit with a memory of Abby.

They were in his truck, the one he used to drive when they had Abby, and she was in the car seat in the back, and he was driving her home from kindergarten. They had stopped at the gas station to get her some candy and a drink. She liked those little Bug Juices and she had gotten a bag of Skittles. She was quiet most of the way home as she dedicated herself to the candy. Dwight watched her out of the corner of the rearview mirror as she fished them out of the bag one at a time. As soon as she had one in her mouth she was eyeing the inside of the bag for the next one. She ate the whole bag, and Dwight remembered wondering what kind of lunch they fed them at school. As she chewed on the last one she held the bag in her hand and looked around the truck. Dwight was not a pig but sometimes he let the truck get a little cluttered, and there was a cup in the floor

and a bag of trash from Taco Bell also in the floor
that day, and on the seat was an old newspaper and
some receipts and another cup, and the dash was
dusty and the windshield had bugs all over it.

Abby eyed the truck and said, "Why is your
truck so dirty? There is trash *everywhere*."

Dwight started to protest but she continued.
She was really talking to herself. She held the Skittles
bag between two fingers. "I'm just gonna throw this
on the floor. It's not like it's gonna matter." And she
held the bag out and let it go, watching it fall to the
floor. Then it dawned on her that she might have
done something wrong and she looked at her daddy,
but he was laughing. He laughed and laughed.

Dwight slammed the door at the memory and
slapped the truck in reverse, revving it into the street
without looking. He stuck it in drive and shoved the
pedal down, hoping they had put up a brick wall at
the end of the street.

When he sat down on his bar stool at The
Shame, he and Belly exchanged hellos, but not much
else. There was a new barfly scoping the place, with
Dennis and a few others. She tried her luck with
Dwight but he ignored her. She flittered over to
Dennis, and an hour later he was practically having
sex with her at the bar. Dwight watched as she
moved around him like a cat in heat. She dropped
her cigarettes and leaned over to pick them up
without bending her knees. She bent over to get
something out of her purse on the floor and
stumbled, and her head landed in his lap. Dwight
stewed in his stool, wondering how far they would go.
Dennis told dumb jokes as he pawed her leg and
draped his arm all over her shoulders. She laughed

her smoker's laugh and drank the drinks he bought her, and acted stupid and slutty. Dennis leaned into her ear and told her something sincere and she ducked her chin and laughed coyly, and then Dennis made his move and had his tongue in her mouth, and she wasn't surprised. Dwight was thoroughly disgusted now to see Dennis had his hand up her shirt groping her little breast as he cleaned the nicotine off her teeth.

"You gonna fuck her right here Dennis?" Dwight asked loudly. Belly looked up from his paper. Dennis backed off of her sheepishly and looked around, as if realizing he was in a bar. "Well no, not here!" He said excitedly, knowing Dwight shared his enthusiasm. He was wrong.

"You just gonna fuck here at the bar, in front of me and Belly and the rest of us, so we can watch? What's her name Dennis, huh?" Dwight's voice rose. Dennis' happy smile turned upside down and his face looked drunk and stupid. "You gonna mount her on the bar, huh, you fucking idiot. Take this stupid whore out in the parking lot and nail her in the gravel where you both belong. Goddamn! Dennis, that's fuckin' disgusting, pawing her in front of everybody like she was a dog. Is that it? You in heat, honey? If we get in line can we all have a go?" The little barfly sat with her mouth slightly open, dismay on her face. "Jesus fuckin' Christ, have some respect for yourself and everyone in viewing distance." Dwight stood up and paid his tab as Belly scowled at him.

"Mother fucker," Dwight said and walked out.

He wasn't really that mad about it, but it irked him. He thought there was no respect left for common rules of society. It was okay to smoke as you walked into the sliding doors at Walmart, blowing smoke in the faces of people leaving the store as you threw your cigarette on the ground without putting it out. It was okay to let your ten-year-old daughter dress with more makeup covering her face than clothes covering her body. It was okay to let your fat little kid sit at his Xbox all day instead of playing outside or doing his homework. It was okay for dad to go to the store with his family Christmas shopping dressed in pajamas, or to wear his baseball cap while he ate dinner at a restaurant. It was okay for a grown man not to have a job. It was okay to pay your bills by collecting unemployment. He thought there had been a time in his life when collecting unemployment was a bad thing, something to avoid. He sighed as he drove home. He did feel a little bit bad though, not about Dennis, fuck him he thought, but he didn't know the woman. He shouldn't have been that mean to her.

The next morning, he was awake early and into the little Kia by 6:15. He drove twenty minutes to the street where Officer Lopez lived. He parked along the curb, two houses down. He wasn't sure what he'd do if someone came up to the car and asked him what he was doing, but he figured people didn't notice much anymore, and just really didn't care. He got out the paper and did the crossword puzzle and smoked while he waited. Two cars left from nearby houses and a couple more went up and down the street, but there wasn't any movement at the Lopez house until 7:15. A white woman with big hips hurried out of the house and got something out of the car and went back in. She looked to be about 40 years old and tired. She was older than Lopez by a few years, maybe 8 or 10, Dwight thought. She was unhappy and Dwight bet he hit her when he thought she needed it.

He wondered why people were content to live unhappy. He and Marlene had gotten married young and had not been in love, not really, he decided. They had really liked each other a lot and had been excited about the idea of being grown up and married, playing house. Their marriage started to falter a little after two years but then they had Abby, and though the baby made the stress and frustration much worse, she was also the glue that held them together. They had something to focus on and work for, together. Marlene had grown up and become responsible and she had dragged Dwight along with her. Neither was really happy, but neither strayed, both worked, and there seemed no change in sight, so they must have been content.

Ten minutes later Dwight saw two of the reasons Mrs. Lopez looked so frazzled, as two raucous little boys about eight and seven rolled out of the house pushing and wrangling each other. They fought for seats in the back, making quite a little stir as mom came out behind them carrying their backpacks, a giant purse and box of something. The boys were darker skinned than mom and seemed to be from Officer Lopez. She tried to get the boys and the stuff settled down in the back and was several minutes doing it. Dwight watched the boys and felt they were okay. They seemed too full of life. No one was shoving them into a closet. The mom got in and started the car and then the door to the house opened and Dwight's gut rumbled as a lithe girl with a book

bag pulled tightly to her chest and long brown hair
falling over her shoulders and covering part of her
face, walked to the car and quickly got into the front
seat. She seemed about thirteen, but might be fifteen,
Dwight couldn't tell. She was wearing faded blue
jeans and a long sleeve shirt on what would be a
warm day. She was white and pale like her mother
and she was not the daughter of Officer Lopez. She
was his step-daughter. And he was having sex with
her. Dwight didn't think she enjoyed having sex with
her step-father.

He gripped the knife beside the seat, thinking
he could go now and plunge it into his throat. He'd
have to catch him by surprise. He might get shot.
The white SUV backed out and left. Dwight sat
poised in his seat, one hand on the door handle and
one hand on the knife for the next minute. If Officer
Lopez had come out of his house Dwight would
probably be dead now. There was no movement at
the house and Dwight relaxed a little as moments
passed. He felt that he should leave. His run as child
molester vigilante would be over soon enough, he
knew, but killing a cop would end it sooner than later.
He thought about following them to the girl's school
and trying to talk her into telling, but scratched that
immediately. She didn't need some strange man
following her at school, talking about being molested.
He thought about confronting the mom. Dwight
imagined the scene as he explained to her that he
knew what her husband was doing to her daughter.
She might believe it; it would certainly plant the idea,
but she would go to her husband first, if she did
anything at all. He might realize who she was talking
about after she described what Dwight looked like,

and he might remember Dwight's name, find his address and pay Dwight a visit.

He took off in the direction of the SUV hoping to find them. He found them toward the head end of a long line of cars trying to turn left on a busy street. He turned left a block sooner, made a right and waited behind two cars as they also tried left turns. He came up to the stop sign and saw the SUV pass in front of him. He sped between cars and got in a car behind them. He followed them for five minutes, staying a car or two behind as she dropped the two boys off at an elementary school. Then it was a ten-minute drive through traffic to let the girl off at her school. Dwight saw the sign in front; Harrison High School. She was probably fifteen and a freshman. Dwight wondered how long it had been going on. He bet it wasn't too long after she started changing with puberty, probably twelve. What a way to spend your young life, Dwight thought. You come home, and you're alone with your intimidating, policeman father figure, and he takes you in the back room and does disgusting things to you, and then you can't even tell your mom. You're afraid of what he'll do to her, to you, or worse afraid she won't believe you. You slink around the house timid and afraid and dirty and she asks "Honey what's wrong? Are you okay?" And you say "Nothing" and wonder how can she not know, why does she not know?

He quit following the mom. He let her go, though he wanted desperately to pull her over and slap the truth into her. He would say to her, "You lure him into the house and get his gun belt off and I'll kill him." He let her go off into her unknown, and he turned for home. He crawled in bed with Dog at 8:30 and slept until the alarm went off.

Dwight mulled it over at work while he washed the toilets and vacuumed the floors. He wasn't going to kill him, though he wanted to and he wondered again how long he'd been at the girl. The thought of little kids being forced to do adult things, alone in a house with someone they trusted, someone they had no control over but who had total control over them, made Dwight furious and desperate to help them. He thought about the first little girl. He'd gotten there just in time, like a hero in the movies, he had saved her. She was alone and helpless against a bad and disturbed man, and just at the moment when he was going to go over the edge, Dwight busted in and stopped him. He felt little goose bumps pop out all over his arms and a warm feeling cruised up and down his body. He teared up and smiled a little. He could spend the rest of his life doing this. He'd track them all down, all the ones he bumped into anyway.

Towards the end of the day, Dwight had finally decided how to handle the cop. He would write a letter, three letters actually; one to his police chief, one to the girl's school principal, and one to the newspaper. He would sit back and watch and read the paper. If that didn't change things, then he would gut him.

He wondered at the plan, how to write the letters, what to write them on, what to say, and how to mail them. He decided to hit the pawn shops again and buy a typewriter or an old computer, print the letters out in simple language, and then throw the computer or typewriter in a dumpster somewhere. Each of the three letters would say the same thing basically. He would say he was affiliated with her school somehow and knew of her abuse by Officer Lopez, but that the girl had not confessed to him. He would say that Officer Lopez needed to be removed from the force and prosecuted, and she needed to be removed from his custody. He would confess himself to not having any proof, but any investigation would lead to the proof. There would be some painful questions asked of Officer Lopez and hopefully, some painful recourse for him as well. He thought about finding out who the school counselor was and following her home and mailing the letters from a box close to her house but decided one near the school would be easier and just as leading.

On the way home, he stopped at a pawn shop and found a word processor with a printer and bought it for fifty bucks, thinking he'd done them a favor. He didn't know how anybody kept up with technology today. Before Abby was born he had a flip phone that he could send and receive fifty texts a month. A few years later he had one that could text, take pictures and perfect video and he could search the internet and communicate with people in ten different ways, and it would tell him how to get from his home to Juno, Alaska, step by step. He was back to a flip phone now.

He stopped at the Walmart on the way home and got some beer and paper for the printer, and a baked chicken, already cooked and hot for five dollars. After thinking about Dog, he went back and got a second chicken. It was amazing to him; a whole chicken, baked in lemon pepper, for five dollars. He hated Walmart and rarely went there, but he had to admit they had the best stuff for the least amount of money. It wasn't always the best quality but it would sure work for the availability and price. *Goddamn Walmart.*

Dwight drank beer and ate chicken with Dog, working on the letter until 10:20. After several beers, he figured now was as good a time as any to mail them. He put on some latex gloves he'd gotten at Walmart and printed them out, enveloped them, and addressed them with the addresses he'd looked up at work. He loaded up Dog and headed over to the school. Once he got there, he drove around for thirty minutes, cursing the whole time until he found a mailbox. He slipped the letters in covertly and drove off, pleased with himself. Even though they were stuffed from the chicken, Dog wanted some sliders so they pulled up to an unsuspecting White Castle on the way home.

As he drove home, Dwight watched Dog stand in the truck seat and eat burgers off the dash. "You landed in dog heaven din'cha, you little fucker? How come you never pay for any of this shit? Jus' cuz I can speak, an I can drive a car and I gotta job, you think I should pay for everything? Huh? I aughta beat your ass." Dog's little nub worked back and forth as he chewed on the little box that had held the little burger. "Good fuckin' dog," he said. Dwight felt pretty good about himself.

Two days later, he hadn't noticed any results, but figured the letters might not have even made it yet. He drove by the Lopez house on his way to The Shame on Saturday and the white SUV was in the driveway and the squad car was gone, but nothing seemed different. He was probably on patrol. *Just hang on, kid.* He looked around the neighborhood and saw no one. Saturday afternoon and there was not a kid outside on the whole street. He remembered on Saturdays, on the street he grew up, the place looked like someone had opened all the cages at the zoo, with kids running around everywhere, dropping down out of trees like monkeys and sprinting back and forth across the street. People drove slower because of the danger of hitting a running child, not because of fear of the law. But now, without any kids in the street, people speed down them unchecked. He drove on by and headed to The Shame.

CHAPTER 9

"You actually seem kinda chipper, Dwight; what's the problem?" Karen asked with a teasing smile as she replaced his drink. "We can't have you smiling up the place." Then she laughed her patented laugh that sounded like a drunken vulture flying off. Dwight smiled within himself. She was a dandy.

"You shut up," was all he could muster. Joni and some of the others laughed.

The bar was getting crowded. It was 8:00 p.m.and the horseshoe part of the bar where Dwight sat was full, and the overflow bar was full, and Belly was helping wash glasses and fill coolers while Joni and Karen ran back and forth. Dwight loved to watch them work as they never got in each other's way, and sometimes they would hear the other get a drink order and fill half of it without the other asking, even as they worked on their own drinks. Every now and then one of them would say, "Belly..." and he'd look over and see they needed more lime slices or a keg changed out or more beer in a cooler, and he'd get on it without them saying anything more. He loved to watch women work when they were determined and busy with what they were doing. It kind of turned him on to watch them, a wisp of hair in their face, especially Karen. Women were more creative and graceful as they worked. They didn't have the muscle to bull through some jobs so they had to cut it into steps and sometimes take the longer but easier way. He also loved to watch them play sports, softball in particular. He liked the way the pony tails stuck out of their caps. He loved that, but he was unsure why he loved it. Marlene had played softball for a couple years after they got married. She was a big girl, and she could hammer the ball. He liked to watch her bat. She looked damn mean. She wore her hat low on her eyes and hunched down a little at the plate, circling the bat gently above her shoulder as she waited for the pitch. She would do it for as long as the pitcher took to deliver the ball. She didn't have a big grunting manly swing either, it was graceful and silent until the bat hit the ball, and then she would sling the bat behind her and thunder down to first. They had sex a lot after games.

He tried to watch Karen now without staring at her. She was young and vibrant, and easy to look at. She was engaging with the patrons, and she talked as much as she worked, always smiling and laughing. She would throw back her head and let out that laugh, loud and unapologetic. One night Dwight had gone out to his car to get a pack of cigarettes and heard Karen laughing in the bar as he leaned into his truck. He thought for half a moment someone was being strangled. He laughed all the way back to his stool. He said loudly to her as he sat down, "I heard you laughing all the way out in the parking lot."

"Yeah? So?," she demanded. Dwight began to feel stupid. "You missed me while you was out there, didncha?"

He recovered enough to say, "People a mile a way don't miss you."

Karen did not dress skimpily or wear anything too tight when she came to work either, but she didn't mind showing some skin. She was always casual sexy. She had some short, cut-off blue jean shorts on tonight with a large metal bottle opener stuck in one back pocket, and a green t-shirt tied up in a knot to allow her belly to show and tennis shoes with no socks on. You could see the head of the chicken peeking out over the top of the front of the shorts. He was like Old Tom. He wanted to see that chicken. He was very content to gaze the length of her legs and watch the hug of her shorts. That bottle opener turned him on. She kept it at the ready there, snugged up next to her butt all night. He liked to watch as she whipped it out and popped the top off a beer and then slammed it back into the pocket against the curve of her rump.

She was a dirty blond and had shoulder length hair she kept in a ponytail stuck through a baseball cap. He liked that. Dwight found himself staring at her as she turned purposely and caught his eye. He was like a deer in the headlights and she loosed a slow smile on him as she sped toward him, grabbed a clean glass, and then turned back to the customer she was chatting with. He looked away and forced himself to look over the other people sitting at the bar.

Dennis was in his usual spot at the stool where the horseshoe bar met the overflow bar and to his right was an older woman in her mid fifties trying to work him over, but even he was having none of that. She was constantly fishing around in a giant purse on her lap for something. *Her life maybe.* To her right were two hefty girls and Dennis *was* trying to land one of those around the older woman, but to her credit, she was blocking him pretty good. She was like Yao Ming the basketball player in the paint, 7 foot 6 and blocking everything, and Dennis was having trouble getting a shot off. Dwight bet the two big girls were happy to have the woman as a buffer. They were on the prowl but they wanted what they would never get. They wanted a cowboy, a real man who had a good job and who loved them, and would snatch them out of their dull and painful lives and whisk them off to his ranch. One who would give them babies and make them happy wives and mothers, despite the truth they were overweight and desperate, which are the two things men dislike the most, because both can easily get worse. That is why there were two of them, so they would not be lonely as they sat at the bar and bought their own drinks. They would not be lonely as they watched the men who would not approach them talk to other women, and so they would not be lonely when they left with each other and stopped at Taco Bell as one of them suggested there might be men leaving the bars there but at that point all they really wanted was some tacos.

To the right of the two ladies, as the bar started to curve, sat a big man Dwight had seen in here only one other time. He was about three inches over six feet, with about three hundred and fifty pounds sticking to his heavy frame. He was intimidating as some big men are just because they are bigger. He was with a dumpy, mouthy woman, who had been talking and smoking since before they even sat down. She and Karen had spoken a few times throughout the night, sounding like two angry squirrels in a tree. He didn't know if they were arguing or just talking, but Karen got louder than usual a few times. Dwight didn't like them. She was on the sad end of forty, skinny, but had a decent, smoke-wrinkled face. What came out of her mouth made Dwight think her ugly. She talked nonstop about everything, loud and right. She blabbed on about politicians, and the cops, and the government, all corrupt and all apparently knew she existed and were out to get her and her man. Her big man didn't say much, sitting there looking tough and dangerous, but he added confirming comments to her tirades at what seemed liked rehearsed moments. She pointed out several times how big and bad he was and bombarded everyone in earshot about how she had been pulled over the other day, and the cop had been all smart and sassy until he leaned in and saw Sambo sitting next to her. Dwight knew the end of the story as soon as she began. Cop acts tough with little woman, cop sees Andre the Giant in the passenger seat, cop gets weak in the knees and falls all over himself trying to apologize and get out of there alive, even though he has the gun. Then there was another awesome story about how he had a pleasant talk with her boss, who was making passes at her at work and blocking her promotion because he wanted to have sex with her, and now she was practically his boss and ran the whole place by herself. They made Dwight angry.

Next to them sat Old Tom and his older wife. Dwight looked her over, shaking his head. She was tired. It looked like Tom had gone back in time to the depression and dragged her away from a bread line, with her finally being one step away from the bread. She always wore scraps of clothing that had been old when she'd bought them used back in the fifties. She had a beaten face, like she lived in a desert. She always wore this lost but not unhappy look, more like confused, but pretty sure everything was okay. She drank the cheapest whisky the bar had from a shot glass, always making sure they didn't try and give her the expensive stuff, and on a long night at the bar she might only have four, as she took a little sip from the shot glass about every half hour.

Dwight watched her in fascination one bored night. He could tell when she was planning to take a drink several minutes before she actually took one when she went to her purse. She would get her old, bag purse off the bar and root slowly around in almost every pocket until she found a worn little blue handkerchief. She seemed like she was looking for other stuff too, but all she ever came up with was that handkerchief. She would pull it out and carefully see that nothing else fell out. Then she would bend over precariously and give a look at the floor. Dwight was sure she'd fall over. Then she would close the purse and put it back on the bar. This done, she would rest a minute or two, sitting there doing nothing, wearing her dull smile, sort of looking around. Then she would dab her lips with the handkerchief. She would crumple the blue rag in her hand and contemplate putting it back in the purse, look at the purse and set a hand on it, but then she would remember she still

needed the handkerchief, and put her hand back in her lap. She would listen to the conversation and smile and nod her head at nothing particular. Then her eyes would make their lazy way to the shot glass, and they would open a little bit in recognition, like remembering a friend was sitting next to her. She would gaze at the glass for some time and then reach out a bony hand for it. She would lean her old head in close and raise the glass about two inches off the bar and bring her lips down to it slowly. Dwight thought it took about as much effort to dock a spaceship to a station in space, slow and careful.
Glass and lips would then meet and she would close her eyes and pull a little sip from the glass, like a fourth of the shot. Eyes still closed, she would set the glass down gingerly. Her eyes would open and her face would flush slightly and a smile would emerge. She would dab her lips again with the ancient blue rag, and then spend the next couple of minutes putting it back in her purse.

Next to them sat two older men he saw in here every now and then. They always came in together and often left with company. They were late forties and pretty good looking, laid back and successful. They were always dressed business casual or for golf. Dwight thought one of them might be married. One time they'd come in with a woman, and she'd treated him in that familiar way, *we're married and we're attached but I really can't stand you.* They had not stayed long that night. Karen knew them both and seemed to be friends with them from somewhere else, and she chatted with them endlessly. Dwight didn't mind them, but he didn't like it when they were in the bar. She called the single one N.D. Dwight found out

from Joni one day that it stood for Neil Diamond.
He would tell the ladies he used to be a stripper, and his stage name was Neil Diamond. Dwight kept an even level of respect for him after hearing that. He and his buddy were into real estate or something.
Tonight they were being eyed heavily by the two heavy hitters but were so far ignoring them. Dwight set his alarm to watch the proceedings around closing if they hadn't found better by then. He thought the girls might just find a quick rodeo to be ridden in if they hung around long enough.

Those two sat at the high point of the horseshoe bar and to their left, four seats away from Dwight, sat a very pretty woman. She was small framed but had a big chest. She had coal black hair that fell all over in the right way. The more she drank, the thicker her Georgia accent got. Her man bounced back and forth between her and the pool table, but after a while he stayed mostly at the pool table. Dwight eyed him a little and noticed he was gambling on the pool, and seemed to be winning. What really impressed Dwight was that he was still friendly with the little group of losers he was beating. Laughter erupted in short bursts as a shot fell in or a game was won. On a couple of his trips to the bar he headed back to the table with a tray of drinks. Take their money, then buy them drinks. His girl was no softy though. She'd been in here before and he had heard the talk around her about when she used to be a police officer a few years ago, and though Dwight believed she had been a cop at one time, he wondered how her career had gone with a fine little frame like that. He thought, with cops and criminals alike trying to nail her it was no wonder she didn't do it anymore.

Sitting next to her, between her and Dwight, sat three young college men, bouncing around, guffawing and telling war stories. Bull shit most of it, Dwight thought. After they jostled into him the second time he said something. Two of them apologized easily enough but the one furthest from him peered down the bar at him with a smirk. Dwight waited for him to get brave enough.

To Dwight's left were two friends of Karen's from her regular job. They were two middle aged ladies who had come to see Karen at her bar. They worked at a pharmaceutical company together. They seemed slightly uncomfortable at first, like they were in the ghetto or something. He thought this might be their first and last visit. They were a silly pair though, after a few drinks, and started to mess with Dwight a little after Karen had introduced them. One was Asian and the other was black. Dwight was glad they sat next to him. It kept Karen coming around to stand and chatter. Dwight loved to listen to her talk. She could gossip and talk about politics, what the celebrities were doing, or what was in the trash can with equal loudness and enthusiasm.

Dwight kept up conversation with Karen's friends to keep her coming around. It wasn't hard; they were out of their element, and he was one of the natives. He asked them how Karen was at work. She was apparently a terror with the management, often letting them know when they messed up. She was a badger at the office and kept everybody on their toes.

Dwight laughed at their stories and put back a few more drinks than usual and began to enjoy himself. He tried to watch Karen's blue jean shorts wiggle around the bar without getting caught but it was more difficult with her friends around. The bar was loud with talk and music and smoke. He looked around but didn't see Belly anywhere. He got bumped again from the college boys and he saw out of the corner of his eye the one sitting next to him turn immediately to apologize so Dwight ignored it, and nothing was said. They were beginning to flirt openly with the former police officer next to them as her man played pool. Dwight could see though she was fending them off without trouble, they were beginning to get too comfortable with her. Old Tom and his wife had left, and the two lonely hearts club ladies had moved next to N.D. and his buddy, and were trying to get ridden home. The loud mouth with her big, fat husband was talking to the bar, to no one in particular, and Dwight found himself listening to what she was saying.

"I'm tellin' you, someone's daddy found out what this mother fucker was doin' to his little boy and he fuckin' killed him. And that's a fact!"

His eyes widened, and he looked around to see who was listening. He felt the whole bar must be listening.

"Someone's daddy went to this guy's house, busted in his front door, and fuckin' killed him, with a knife! I ain't a shittin' ya, eight times wasn't enough." *Eight times? I stabbed him eight times?* She blew out her cigarette smoke and crushed the butt in an ashtray as her idiot husband added something.

"I'd a cut his ball off and stuffed 'em in his mouth. And then sat there while he choked on 'em. Then I'd a cut his fuckin' head off and took it home

with me and mounted it on my deer wall!" He
finished proudly.

"Ha, ha! He would have done that! That guy's
lucky Sambo didn't kill him, his head would be
hanging in his man cave right now!" She laughed at
her magnificent man.

"That's sad, though, about that one kid," the
ex cop said. "Did you hear about the one in high
school who came out and said he'd been molested by
that guy while he was in that day care?"

Dwight shuddered inside as he awaited. Loud
mouth jumped in before the lady could finish.

"Oh Yeah! He hung himself." Her big man
nodded his head, and then Karen's friends gasped.
"He's been messed up since daycare, in and out of
hospitals and seeing therapists and shit. He never
told his parents what happened at the daycare though.
He was kicked out of junior high for starting fires, but
he was doing okay in high school, he'd been doing
better, but then the news came out about this guy got
murdered and it all came back to him. He was the
first one that told about the abuse and then he
couldn't handle it and he hung hisself in his room just
this morning before he was supposed to go to
school." She finished with flair and sat back to enjoy
the attention. Dwight looked at her in disgust. This
young man had had his pants pulled down and his
childhood ruined, and spent his whole life feeling
wrong to the point he finally couldn't take it anymore,
and this woman was getting her legs wet with the
telling of it all. *Stupid cow.*

"That's terrible!" the ex cop said sadly. "His
parents must be sick, so sick." She said the last part

softly, deeply affected. "How can you recover from that? You can't!"

"No you can't," the big man stepped up and said. "That boy's in a better place now." The bar was silent as everyone at the bar was listening for a moment. And then he went and capped off his brilliance by saying reverently and softly, "God works in mysterious ways."

More silence at the bar and some nodding heads. Dwight's cigarette fell from his mouth and flopped on the bar.

"What did you just say?" He said it loud and clear and suddenly there was a new air in the bar. Dwight waited. Surely, he hadn't said that.

Belly walked in from the back with a tray of glasses and began putting them out. The big guy straightened up and looked Dwight in the eye. "God does things for a reason, things we don't understand. That poor boy is in heaven with God and that pervert is in hell, getting' fucked by the devil!" He looked around for confirmation and found silence. Belly looked around the bar sensing he had missed something. The room had become uncomfortable. Serious talks about God and the devil were left to the preacher and those talks were all one way. You could sleep through those talks. No one had open talks with strangers or friends about what God did.

Dwight boiled up inside and the heat blew out of his mouth.

"You think God did that? You think God had that boy's parents put him in a daycare, had a grown man molest him and abuse him when he was a little defenseless thing, and then you think He let that little boy spend the rest of his life in a living hell, so he could find out later that the man that had molested him had been stabbed to death so it would remind him of what he had finally been able to block out that he *had* been molested and then He had him tell his parents about it, so they probably went ape shit and might not even have believed him, and *then*, you think God had this boy kill himself in his own house so his parents could find their molested son hanged, and you think God did all of this so he could GET THAT LITTLE BOY UP IN HEAVEN WITH HIM?" By the end Dwight was yelling and the whole bar became quiet. The ladies next to him were stunned; Karen and Joni were silent and unsure what to do. The big man kept his eyes locked on Dwight, at first unable to respond, so Dwight prompted him again. Belly started toward Dwight with his hands up, but it was way too late.

"WELL? You fucking idiot. Is THAT the mysterious ways you were talking about?"

"Hey! That is not what he meant and you know it!" His wife fumed and pointed her finger at Dwight. "God does things, and we don't know why!"

He finally stood up, angry and huffy, and said, "Hey, asshole! I don't know why that happened to those little kids but God didn't *let* it happen, I didn't say that. He did put a stop to it! I *know* he did that!"

"That was just a sick, sick man who did that those children, Dwight," one of Karen's friends said. "But that man's right, Dwight. I believe He did work through the man that put an end to it. When people say *He works in mysterious ways*, it means we don't understand why things happen, but it is all part of His plan for us, we just can't see the whole picture. Do you see?"

"Just let it go and have another drink, man," the frat boy at the end said contemptuously.

"Shut your mouth, boy." Belly said to him, then he looked at Dwight and said, "Maybe it's time to go man."

Dwight ignored him and started to regret saying this as he said it, knowing it would probably ruin everyone's night. He was still talking to the big dumb guy but he felt like he was speaking to everyone. "I can see part of the picture pretty clearly. I see little children being abused and no one there to stop it. And then you have the nerve to think that God put a stop to it after *fifteen years*? Was he bored of watching?"

There was a collective rumble at this last remark. The ladies next to him made faces and immediately began to gather their things, but Dwight said fuck it, why not? He looked at big dummy and his wife.

"There is NOTHING *mysterious* about the things we do to each other. If you take God out of it then all you have left is a man with bent desires who was able to fool parents that trusted him, and do things to their kids that NO ONE should be allowed to do, and he did it for *fifteen years*, and no one stopped him until one day this guy found out and he was mad enough to kill him for it. GOD didn't help him. GOD didn't guide his hand with the knife. There was one guy doing something really bad and there was another guy who stopped him. God didn't do a fucking thing to start it or stop it. You prance around with your big fat ass and your fucking loudmouth sidekick spreading stupid all over the place. I'm fucking tired of it, so why don't you both just shut the fuck up?" And then Dwight was ready to leave realizing he looked like an angry fool. He had spit his venom everywhere, all over everybody, and it was enough. He was willing to let it go and forget the whole thing, but he knew he had gone too far. He said all this in a loud but even voice. He had the attention of most of the bar and he was mad but he was calm. He got out a cigarette and began to light it, waiting.

"You watch your fuckin' mouth." The big man was getting up and he was mad.

His wife said, "You got some problems, man! You need to go to church," and she laughed a nervous laugh.

"I'll watch my fuckin' mouth if you shut yours, fat boy," Dwight said looking at him.

"There's somebody here who needs his mouth shut, but it ain't him." The college boy spoke up again and Dwight decided his time had come.

"Well come around from behind your boyfriends and do it then." Dwight got up and advanced past the first two frats as they melted against the bar. He was at the young man, who stood up nervously.

"Dwight!" Belly yelled at him.

Dwight then heard what he knew would happen, what he had been waiting for, as the man started around the bar and said, "Hey, Buddy, why don't you pick on somebody your own size!"

Dwight stared evenly at the frat boy, but said to him, "You're not my size, fat boy, but you just keep fucking coming." He left the frat who sat back down and he started around to meet him, when a hand shot out from the bar and grabbed him firmly by the arm.

He thought the young frat boy was grabbing him and started to let hell loose, but as he looked down he saw the painted fingernails and the smooth woman's arm and he looked into to the face of the ex cop.

"Now, I think you should just go back to your seat, there's no need for any of this!"

Dwight paused a moment, thrown off. He was all set to beat on big dummy, he was ready to go, but this nice, slight woman suddenly had a hold of him and he certainly wasn't going to fight with her.

Belly tried again. "Dwight, c'mon man, sit back down."

"Hey, what the fuck are you doing man?" About that time her boyfriend showed up from his pool game, and he was not happy. And here was big dummy finally within distance and as Dwight was distracted by two other people, he lunged with both fists swinging. Dwight was stunned he would swing so close to this lady, but she still held his left arm and all he had free was a broken hand with a cast on it.

He swung straight out with his broken right hand into the fat man's sternum. Both of the man's fists landed clumsily on Dwight's head but without much power. Dwight's punch forced the wind out of him but it did not stop his momentum, and he crashed heavily into Dwight and the weight was more than he could bear. He fell back into the cop's husband as he approached, but he sidestepped and then pushed Dwight hard away from him as they fell. Dwight slammed into the floor and immediately felt painful blows to his body and realized that frat boy was kicking him. He was about to grab one of his legs and pull him down when he heard a loud yell and saw Karen come over the bar with a beer mug, which she landed on the college boy's head with a loud BONK. She fell awkwardly and hard against a table and then onto the floor and Dwight saw her unable to get up, and that was enough. He raised up like a cat on fire and hit the frat hard in his mouth, spinning his head and body around, and he careened into the side of the bar and went down to the floor. Next, he turned to the ex cop's man to see if he wanted some, but he was backing away so Dwight quickly took two steps toward the big man who was already coming his way, and Dwight punched him in the sternum again, but hard this time; he wanted to break something. He let out a loud "whoof" and bent over as he stumbled back, clutching his chest. Dwight hit him high up on his cheek bone as hard as he could, and he went on over backward, crashing into a table full of people and drinks, spilling and breaking things everywhere.

He heard a woman's loud voice yell in his ear and he felt something hard pressed against his head.

"YOU!" She roared.

"Whoa! Whoa!" Belly yelled coming from around the bar.

"Don't you ever touch my husband! NEVER!" she hissed.

Dwight stopped and raised his hands slightly. He felt the gun shaking against his head and he thought she might shoot him on accident or on purpose at any moment. She was behind him but moved to come face to face with him, and as she did he grabbed her right hand with his left and clubbed her on the side of the head as hard as he could with his cast hand. She reeled and dropped to the floor. Dwight went quickly to her and crushed her hand with his foot until she let go of the gun. Nobody moved as he stood up. He walked over to Karen and she got up as he helped her.

"You okay?" he said softly.

She nodded her head. "Yeah." She was shaking. He wanted to grab her and hold her.

"Thanks." He said and smiled at her.

He walked over and got his cigarettes and lighter. The frats had gathered their friend and were already leaving. One of them looked at Dwight and gave an apologetic shrug. Besides general straightening, no one else moved. His eyes met Belly's behind the bar. Belly reached down and grabbed the phone, still looking at Dwight. Dwight frowned and shrugged. *Oh well.* He set the gun down over the bar by the glasses and walked out.

He rested his head on the steering wheel and laughed a short sad laugh. *What the fuck is going on?* He quickly started the truck and left.

CHAPTER 10

He pulled into the White Castle parking lot with his mind still going over the events at The Shame. He wondered if Belly had had enough. *He might not let me back.* This thought stopped him. He had caused quite a bit of trouble there, but he was the most regular customer Belly had. He would go in Monday after work and have a talk with him. He wouldn't start any more fights. He'd had enough. He had plenty to do anyway. He needed The Shame. He couldn't start over again.

He shut the engine off and suddenly wondered why he had parked in the White Castle parking lot and not gone through the drive through. *Oh well.* He'd go inside. He walked to the door thinking about the fight, and Karen, and a waft of the smell hit him as he reached for the door, and he felt a knotting in his stomach. He jerked his hand back like he'd been shocked. The smell of rot and sewer lingered at the door, his stomach turned over and he looked around for garbage or vomit or whatever, but he knew. He stepped back and bent over, putting his hands to his knees and hung his head over, tired and revolted. *Why? I can't even get something to eat without this?*

Then he thought the funeral, grabbing Abby while she lay in the casket, and he suddenly remembered again the first time a faint smell of rot around her he had ignored before because it was so disgusting. He had refused to associate it with her. He remembered the first hint of that smell and then blocked it out. Associating it with her now made his stomach twist and roll over and the smell around the door made him dizzy. *Fuck this.* He turned quickly and walked back to his truck. He could no longer smell it and he leaned his head over the side of the truck breathing heavily. As he rested his head there, he looked at the contents of his truck bed; an old screwdriver, a half empty quart of oil, two beer cans, some loose tie down string and a bungee cord. And then up under his tool box almost hidden in the darkness and shadows cast by the parking lot lights, he saw two bricks. For a painful few moments he remembered he used to be a bricklayer, with a wife and a house and a bunch of payments and some friends and a bunch of stuff piled up in the garage where his cars should have been, and a little girl. A little girl. While he sat inside and played a kid's game, when he should have been watching her climb trees and dance around the backyard, someone took her and broke her. He climbed into the back of the truck and got the two bricks out and climbed back out. He turned the bricks over in his hands and then threw them under some bushes. He looked back at the restaurant and said softly, "Okay Baby. Okay."

He couldn't go inside as he would probably throw up everywhere and cause a scene. He walked around the parking lot looking the cars over, and as he approached a lime green Geo he began to smell it. The car looked several years old but clean. He got closer and saw a bumper sticker with a cross on it reading "God Resides at Oakville Baptist Church." He paused, looking at the sticker and wondered if God knew he resided at Oakville Baptist Church, and if He knew what one of the faithful in His favorite church was doing with some of His little children. He remembered the talk of God at the bar and he sighed. How could people think God had anything to do with their actions, good or bad? He found his mouth was full of saliva and he spit it on the back of the car. He walked over to his truck and sat inside.

A few minutes later a skinny man of medium height walked out of the White Castle holding a white bag and plodded to the Geo. He was about 40 years old. He got in and started the car and immediately Dwight saw the reverse lights come on. He backed up and sped off quickly out of the parking lot, and Dwight followed.

They drove about three miles through the city with Dwight close behind. He didn't care if the guy thought he was being followed. A guy like him would still drive straight home, wondering the whole time if he was being followed.

They pulled into an apartment complex and Dwight saw he was parking and he pulled off and parked a few spaces away. He got out of his truck and followed not too far behind him as he plodded to his apartment. He glanced nervously back at Dwight as he went up the stairs. Dwight followed, their footsteps ringing softly in the stairwell. He risked a glance at Dwight when the steps turned. Dwight looked him in the eye flatly and followed. At the 2nd story landing he got his keys out and went to the door on the right, risking another glance. Dwight turned to the door on the left and felt the man relax, though hurrying with his keys. The moment the door began to open Dwight soft toed up behind him and pushed him through the door. They wrestled for a brief moment but Dwight easily put him in a choke hold and squeezed hard. He drug him over to the door and closed and locked it.

Dwight said quickly, "I'm not going to rob you or hurt you. I need something from you and once you give that to me I will go. Do you understand?" He squirmed and whimpered, flailing around vainly, but seemed to understand and he began to settle down. "I'm going to let you go in a second, and the moment you yell or get your phone out or do anything but sit the fuck down quietly, I will hurt you, and I will hurt you bad. I don't really care either way. Do you wanna get hurt bad or sit quietly?"

He relaxed the pressure a little and waited a few seconds. He sniffled and gasped and sobbed and Dwight was just about to say fuck it when he cried, "Sit quietly."

He let him go and pointed to the couch like he would to a dog or a child. He sat down on the couch adjusting his glasses and sniffling, looking furtively around his apartment. Dwight thought, *do something.*

"Yell out or get up to grab something." Dwight eyed him to calmly.

He looked at Dwight, trying to collect himself and appear brave or something. But he stammered, "Wh-what do you want?"

Dwight looked at him, all skinny and soft, wide eyed and pale behind his glasses. Beneath that was some cunning though, like a rat waiting at the edges of the fray. He had an air about him of weird authority, almost starting to dismiss Dwight as he glanced away. He looked back at Dwight, *well?*

Dwight became a little uncertain. How did he know if this guy molested choir boys? So he stank like the shit all over Huckson, the daycare guy. So he had that same puke death smell that came off Abby. Maybe it was the smell of bad things that had happened to that person. Or when something bad happened like that, the smell was on both people. He looked him over again and felt, no he knew, this fuck had done something. Maybe it was done to him at some time and that was bad for him, but now he was passing it on. Isn't that how it happened? The abused became the abuser?

"You work at the church?" It was an odd first question for a break-in he knew, but it was all he could think of.

The man looked up at Dwight. "Yes." The response had a note at the end of it saying the obvious, what could that ever in the world have to do with your breaking in here? But it was too delayed. Too long and drawn out. He had to emphasize what was already obvious. There was something there.

"What do you do?"

"Well...I am The Choir Instructor." Like that was an actual title or something.

Dwight waited and said nothing.

"Boys Choir," Dwight said. A statement, not a question.

And there it was. A flustered look, glancing left and right, looking at nothing, finger pushing up glasses already pushed up, fidgeting.

He began, "Yes, the boys ch-" but Dwight cut him off.

"I've had a talk with some of the boys." More pause to let that sink in. "And the one thing I need from you is kinda an easy thing. It'll change your life around some, you'll have to adjust this and that, but it's not really all that bad. Considering."

He wouldn't look at Dwight now and he seemed to be sweating. He looked down at the floor and rocked a little. "*What* are you talking about?"

"Let's don't play this game, ok? I know, and it's a pretty serious thing, huh? Molesting little boys." It was out there now. Before he got all huffy, Dwight said quickly, "But that one little thing I need from you is not that serious. It's an easy thing and it solves all our problems. You want to hear that little thing?" Dwight waited.

He sat mousy, wondering what was happening, looking for the exit from this mouse trap. He rubbed his hands, kind of pressing them into his crotch. It was almost more than Dwight could stand and he was about to tell him to quit fucking doing it when he stopped. "I don't understand," he said pleadingly, "what boys did you talk with? I'm not inappropriate with any of the boys in my choir. I play games with some of them. We play games, as a reward, for being good. They like it. You have to be good, to play the games, so why would they behave if they didn't want to play? There's nothing wrong with it, we just play games."

"Some people, well everyone actually, calls that child molestation. Can we move on now? It's an easy little thing. Are you ready to hear it?"

"I am The Choir Instructor and I teach them how to sing! That's all I do. We play games that's all! As a reward for trying hard and paying attention and behaving, they get to play games…"

He was trying to convince Dwight, but he was almost speaking to the open air, trying to convince himself, maybe. Dwight was a little uncertain now and beginning to regret being here. He felt like a counselor, and all he really wanted to do was kill someone who molested kids. But the smell was everywhere, wafting all over the place. Dwight was breathing through his mouth but it was like standing in a garbage heap, or dirty slaughterhouse. The sting of the smell was in his eyes, in his brain. He could not stay here much longer.

"Games, huh? That's what you call it? Wrestling? Tickling? Does that make it easier for you? How often do you accidently touch their dick, or push their hand onto yours? Back rubs? I know some of it, but they didn't like to talk about it, and I didn't press them. But I can.
I will. But I thought, let's just end this thing. I'll go and have a talk with him and make him realize his behavior *is* wrong, he *is* being inappropriate, but maybe he just doesn't realize it, huh? So here I am, telling you, you are a child molester. The things those boy told me you do to them is *child molestation*. You're not fucking certain? If you and I wrestle around right now and I touch your dick I'm telling you I want to

fuck you, understand? When you do that to a kid, it's called child molestation. But I've got a deal for you, partner. I'm tired of fucking being here. I wanted to go to the police but those boys love Jesus ,and they didn't want everyone to know, so I said I'd make you quit and that would be that, no one would know, and we'd be done. That's it. That's the little thing, you just need to resign. I can easily go and tell the cops, or better yet, tell their parents, which is what I should've done instead of coming here. I can tell their parents, and their parents will get it out of them, and then the national news will land upon you and your church and you'll probably get a free ride to the goddamn prison, which incidentally, I hear, is not a nice place for pedophiles, just saying. So, this is your option, quit that fucking church for whatever reason, and move away."

All this time the choir instructor had slowly melted into the coach, just listening, but he went wide eyed at the mention of moving away.

"You think that's too drastic? Quitting *and* moving away? Well say no then, just say the fuck no."

He leaned back into the couch and exhaled loudly, like he was dying. He took his glasses off and covered his face with his hands and he leaned forward and cried a little. "I have been the Choir Instructor at Oakville Baptist Church for four years. I have been good to those boys. I have loved those boys like they were my own. Little Brothers, I called them. My Little Brothers Choir…Who has said these things about me? I must know. I will resign…and move away, if I must. If it will save the church such a terrible scandal, but I must know which of my boys has misunderstood and thinks I have been so wrong to them."

Dwight went hot. This little fuck was going to be a martyr, huh? Going to sacrifice himself to save the church? *Fuck this.*

"Which ones? *You* tell me." Dwight leaned over the coffee table and hit him hard in the face. He yelled out and slammed into the couch, then slowly fell onto his side, making whimpering sounds and covering his face. Dwight went around the coffee table and hit him in the exposed side of his face hard again. He bounced off the cushion a little and tried to get up, get away, but Dwight grabbed him by the hair and drug him onto the floor. He got on top of him and lifted his head off the floor by his hair and hit him again and again. Blood mingled with snot and flowed from his nose; his mouth started to bleed onto his teeth. His eyes wandered around unfocused.

"How 'bout *you* tell *me*? Tell me their names and what you did to them and I won't kill you." Dwight began to get sick from the ever-present stench and watching the fluids mingle on this guy's face. He found a sweater on a chair and grabbed it. He dragged over his face, roughly cleaning it off. "Tell me the special ones you play games with and what you do to them in those games. After you've told me I'll leave. You can call the police if you want, I don't mind, then I can get this out in the public where I want it. But if you'd rather, you can write a letter to the church and resign because you've found your true calling in another state. Then you can move and call it a day."

Dwight gripped his hair tightly and started to lift his head off the floor again.

"Jason!" he spluttered quickly. "Jason…um. Travis. Michael, uh oh my god. Uh…Steven." He paused and acted like he might pass out. Dwight slapped him. Just guessing, he said, "And?"

He groaned, stunned from the slap. "Ohhh! Damian. That's all of them. Just those."

"And the games?"

He kept his eyes closed as if speaking to himself. "We play Wii. We play games on the Wii, tennis and boxing. They think it's fun. None of them have a Wii. If they lose, I get to tickle them. I'm good at Wii. I make them wear loose shorts without underwear, so they can play the Wii better, so when i tickle them I can…"

Dwight pulled the knife out from behind his back and drove it into the side of his neck. He jerked and his arms flailed out, and his eyes bugged out. Dwight got up. He wriggled around on the floor and tried to regain himself, one hand tenderly groping the knife, but he could not get up. He sighed a painful sound and gurgled blood. Dwight stood over him. He opened and closed his mouth like a fish, gasping.

Dwight bent down close and put his check next to his. He could feel the stubble of his own face, rough against the man's smooth skin, his eyes squeezed shut with tears dripping out.

"I don't know any of the boys in your choir. I do know you were molesting someone, I just guessed at the rest. I needed to hear you say it so I could kill you."

He suddenly smelled the smell all over him and he looked at what he'd done and he realized he had enjoyed some of it. He was nauseous with it all, and he vomited on the man's chest and neck. He gasped and spit the last of it out and wiped his mouth. He looked down in disgust and he knew he would not clean that up, even if it led the police to him, who *fucking* cared? He was not cleaning that up.

He got up and went for the door. He turned the knob but the door would not open. He looked at the knob stupidly for a moment and then noticed he had put the deadbolt on. He grabbed it with the bottom of his shirt and turned it. Then he grabbed the handle with his shirt and opened the door. He neither saw nor heard anyone as he walked back to his truck. He might not have seen them if he'd walked right past them. He didn't know if anyone saw him. He got into his truck like a robot and drove off. He drove down the lighted streets past open and closed stores, through intersections, stopping at stop signs, going through greens and yellows and stopping at reds and he saw none of it. He had both hands on the wheel and his mind had both hands locked around his thoughts, squeezing them, forcing them to remain quiet.

He sagged in the truck seat and leaned forward a little as he drove, and then one thought finally forced its way past like a bubble in a tar pit and broke free to say, "Where is the knife?"

He braked hard in the middle of the street and adrenaline surged through him. "Oh fuck!" he moaned. "Oh fuck!" He pulled into a strip mall parking lot and came to a stop somewhere in the middle.

"You stupid motherfucker! Go around killin' people and leave the goddamn *knife* shoved into their fucking throat! With yer fuckin' fingerprints all over it…" he slumped his head against the wheel. "Let's

just go to jail…and get raped in prison…and goddamn…by the same *fucking people who killed Abby!*
 Nooo! That ain't gonna happen. There'll be some motherfuckers die before that happens." He raised his head and looked around. That would definitely not happen. He wondered what to do.

Go get the knife.

Well why not? He looked around the strip mall to see where he was. Shit, he was miles away. He put it in gear, thinking as he went. There'd be no one there. Nobody would find that pervert until the rent didn't get paid. And he'd still be dead.

He made his way back to the area and after going up and down some streets, he finally located the apartment complex and pulled into the same parking spot. He got out quickly and walked back up the stairs to the door and after a brief hesitation, thought *fuck it*, and turned the handle. It opened easily and in a moment, he was inside with the door shut looking at a stiff body with vomit and blood all over it and a huge knife sticking out of the side of the neck. Grabbing his nerve by the reins, he went over to the body and put his foot against his head and pulled on the knife. It was stuck tight. He pulled again and heard a little squishing sound and a couple of cracks like bones chipping and he was afraid for a moment that he was gonna shove the head clear off the body as he pushed with his foot, when the knife finally sucked free and he fell backward a little. He stood up and looked around the apartment. *What else?* He saw nothing else that he could, or would, do here. He listened and heard nothing impending. He grabbed the door with his sleeve again and left.

In his truck again, he drove toward his home, one hand on the wheel and the other laying limp in the seat, his eyes blank and his face dull, the knife laying on the seat next to him, doing the speed limit and making all the right stops. He was numb, so numb he only registered dimly that if he got into a wreck he might not notice. The lights of the signs and stores, and the other cars passed by him, as he sat still in the seat of the truck motionless, but for a slight move of his arm on the wheel or a shift of his foot.

There were three of them. He had killed three people. Murdered them. They were dead, and he had done it, brutally, taken a knife and run them through, crushed their face with his fist. Three men, with families and kids and sisters and mothers, who were now all crying and wondering *why oh why this?* And there were cops looking around and writing stuff down and making files and asking questions. *Holy Jesus fucking Christ.* How many people do you need to kill before you're a serial killer? *Two probably, separate ones, not really connected in any way, except they're prostitutes, or old people.* Well he was in there now, not big time but one day there'd be something on TV about this loser who killed three guys as they minded their own business. And they'd go over what he'd done and how they'd caught him and how he died from lethal injection after spending twelve years on death row. And he'd be yelling how they had it coming, and they'd go over how he had come to such an end. They'd talk about Abigail on TV again, and they'd review what had been done to her, in detail, because they had to.

He had both hands on the wheel now, trying to choke it to death, and the lights and cars were speeding by, and he looked at the speedometer and saw why. He let his foot off the gas and let his breath out and sank back down into his seat. *They did have it coming. They* did *have it coming.* He forced himself to breathe slowly.

And I'm gonna do it again.

All the way home, he thought about himself and what he had become. He thought about weapons; guns and knives and pliers and hammers, torches and gasoline, and he imagined dragging men out in the woods and hanging them upside down in trees and shooting arrows into their crotch and building fires under them. He would get them to confess and he would write it all down and pin it to them with a nail after they were dead and leave them to be found.

People would say, "Oh my, he can't do that. Grown men that pull little kids into closets and rape them repeatedly shouldn't have to suffer like that. It's not right. They should be put in prison for 200 years where they can find Jesus and write children's books and get law degrees and become famous and get a whole cult following of people who say, 'Look at this man now. He has been reformed, he has found Jesus, and he is so special and undeserving of any more punishment.'" *Jesus must hide in prison, 'cause people are always finding him in there.*

That's why we can't let em go to jail, he thought. *We should be cutting their dicks off and putting them on a string around their necks and branding their foreheads with big* M's. *Attention everyone, this person is bad and you have the social right and obligation to be mean to them and treat them like dirt. And they have the right to grovel around on the ground and be remorseful and hope no one throws rocks at them.*

He felt a rumble in his belly, the porcupine moving, unhappy about something and needing to readjust. He gritted his teeth and felt the pain, but it was not there anymore. As soon as he turned right onto his street, he realized he hadn't gotten anything to eat. *Oh damn.* He was just hungry. He sighed in relief. He thought about what he had to eat at home and imagined the look on Dog's face when he poured a can of green beans into a bowl.

Since he was already home he pulled into the drive to get Dog. He grabbed the knife and went into the garage, looking around. He found a shop rag and then another and wrapped both of them around the knife. Then he found a cereal box in the trash can and stuffed the wrapped up knife into it, putting trash in with it. Then he buried it in the trash can and went in the house to get Dog. Dog met him at the door, salivating and wiggling all over the place and noticing there was nothing to eat in his hands. But then he began to sniff him furiously, and Dwight stopped and watched him. He combed every inch he could reach with his nose. *He knows.* After he was done, he stood looking up at Dwight. "You done? C'mon stupid." He held open the door and Dog understood immediately and was at the truck before Dwight shut the house door. "We aint getn sliders ya god damn dog. We're going to the grocery store and you're gonna hafta sit in the truck and donchoo say a fuckin thing about it."

Dwight was too wound up to go back home and sleep. They needed groceries anyway. As he drove, he thought how surreal it all was, killing people and then going grocery shopping with your dog. He didn't think about the part of himself that had been destroyed, the part he hadn't been watching, the hollow part that would never be repaired. For the eight minutes it took to drive to the store he pulled on Dog's ear until Dog looked at him like "what the hell?" He said stupid things to him, and petted him. He felt good about some of the things he had done lately and he had his best friend with him, just driving around. He was as happy as he would never be again.

CHAPTER 11

The Country Mart was not as close as the
Walmart, and not as far away as the Hy-Vee, but it
was definitely the worst of the three grocery stores. It
was small and old and just seemed dirty, though it was
actually pretty clean. The meat seemed old and was
always discounted, and the ice cream freezer was
loaded with the cheapest brands of ice cream. Some
of it you sort of had to chip loose from the frost, like
an iceberg of ice cream. It was a 24-hour store and
no matter when you went in there, it had the 2:00 am
people walking around in it, zombies of humankind,
alive in form but dead inside. Trench coats and
nurses' scrubs and pajamas was Country Mart black
tie, or maybe they just gave you a discount for
dressing midnight casual. There were cracks and
missing pieces in several of the floor tiles and the old
lighting still had some of the ancient bulbs and they
gave off a creepy, sick yellow glow, some of them
flickering, and if you really wanted to read what you
were buying you had to bring one of those headlamps
or use the light on your phone.

After Abby's death, when Dwight had sort of been able to stand on his own again, and he had totally moved out of the house and into the rent house, this Country Mart was the first place he applied to for work. He thought if he could do anything, he could probably stock groceries in the middle of the night with the zombies, quiet in their dull shopping. They called him that afternoon after he had applied and gone home, and they wanted him to work the day shift collecting the grocery carts from the parking lot and assisting the checkers as needed, and then pretty soon they would move him up to checker. He was mildly annoyed with the guy calling, as he had only checked the night shift box on the application and he told the guy so, sort of pissed off like, but he persisted without getting mad, telling him he knew with Dwight's background he would be checker soon and who knew after that? They were always needing managers. Dwight paused, a little confused, while all the man had said sifted into his brain. The softness in the man's voice registered finally, and Dwight knew he had talked to somebody on his application and they had told him something of what had happened. He almost unloaded on him over the phone and he imagined going down to the store and shoving the daylight job up his ass, but he stopped, knowing he had to have a job. He had to get back into life, or just check out completely, and so far, he hadn't done that yet. He didn't know why. Somewhere, though he knew it was cowardly and somewhere inside of him, he wanted to be alive to feel the pain.

The man was still silent, waiting for Dwight to speak. And he heard in his mind again the compassion in his voice as he had explained the job, trying to make the job of collecting carts at a third-world grocery store appealing, and Dwight realized he was not really trying to fill an open position. He was holding out a hand to a man he hadn't met. A manager at a dumpy grocery store in a poor part of town was holding out what little he had to give to a man he pitied, and Dwight felt this coming through over the phone and he choked up. Shame washed over him and he gripped the phone with all his strength hoping it would shatter, wanting to smash it against the coffee table. *Don't be nice to me you stupid fuck!* He put the phone down on the table and knelt on the floor. He forced everything out of his mind and tried to pull himself back. His eyes squeezed tightly shut on their own holding it all inside. He blew his nose on his shirt and wiped his eyes. He stood up and grabbed the phone.

"Thank you, um for that offer but I can't. I need to work at night, for my schedule." *What schedule?* He paused unable to say more at the moment, hoping the guy wouldn't do anymore. *Just let me go.*

From then on Dwight only shopped at the Country Mart. He blinked his eyes in the pale glow of the store as he walked down the aisles, looking at the billions and billions of choices.

The next day at work, he emptied the trash cans from the 2nd floor, constantly trying not to think about last night. He managed except for one thought that came floating through, and it seemed to be a good idea. He felt he should write a letter on his word processor to the Oakville Baptist Church and let

them know The Choir Instructor would not be able
to make it in anymore. He was now Satan's Choir
Instructor. He thought the boys might need some
counseling or something. Someone should know they
had been abused, so they didn't have to hold that in
all their lives. *And commit suicide later*, Dwight thought.

But if he did that, he thought it would probably
provide the police with a link between the murders
and the letters about the police officer. He really had
no end game here, but he didn't want to go to prison
just yet, or ever, so maybe the less information for
them was best. He sort of wanted everything to be
over for him. Not suicide, but just done. A shootout
with the police wouldn't happen because he would
just surrender, and then go to jail, which he didn't
want. Suicide would be hard on others. His dad and
brother, though he didn't really care about them,
Dog, and even Marlene. Just another bad thing in her
life. He still might do it though. He could go hunting
and fall out of a tree and shoot himself on the way
down. He thought about that some. He used to hunt
and people could believe that. He kept it in reserve.

Maybe he could just write a letter and say he
was a concerned party, and he heard from one of the
boys that the choir instructor was playing
inappropriate games with some of his them, and he
could list their names so they might talk with them.
At least the parents would know. He could threaten
to tell the police if the parents weren't made aware of
the allegations. He would say nothing about the
death. He thought about that for a minute and
realized it was good enough. He didn't really care to
do more to protect himself. Then he thought that
could be his thing, maybe. He could be like Clark

Kent. He would smell the people out then investigate their lives. He would already know they had committed the crime, then he would just have to prove it, or prove enough of it to cause a scandal. He could be like a superhero journalist stopping child molesters with the written word, and then he wouldn't have to kill anyone else. Their lives would be ruined and they would be found out and go to jail. He straightened up and paused, letting that thought stew. A grimace settled in on his face as he thought of these people denying the allegations and making a big spectacle out of the trial, and then getting off with a good lawyer. Becoming famous. Getting their own reality TV show.

He put a trash can down with a bang, startling a man at the elevator.

"Fuck that," he said to himself, putting a new bag in the can.

He went about the rest of his day efficiently but slowly, letting his mind wander around harmless topics, like Karen's butt. He should work on that a little more. He knew she liked him some, and he knew if he did it right she would probably go out with him. The problem was he really didn't know how to do it right. She was like an alley cat. If you really wanted to pet it, it wouldn't get anywhere near you. Maybe he should throw rocks at her. He laughed at that. That would be a good way to get hurt.

The smile faded from his face as he realized he couldn't get close to her. What would be the point? If she gave herself to him, it would be all of her. She would go all in if she trusted him. And then the cops would bang down their newly painted door, and she would discover he was a serial killer, and her world would go to shit, and she would get to live with that the rest of her life, fucking up all of the rest of her relationships, hating him. His face soured and he sighed. He forgot about her butt and buried his mind in the trash.

He waded slowly through the next few weeks. He worked and drank and fed Dog. He did a few repairs on the house and even had a brief thought of putting a brick patio over the old cracked concrete one. But that was what he used to do. He didn't know if he had that in him anymore. He read the paper occasionally and found that Officer Lopez had been suspended with pay and the daughter was moved into a foster home during the investigation. He tried not to find out any more news about it, hoping the girl would tell the truth, and the mom would see the truth and he would go to jail. But he was afraid none of that would happen, so he didn't look. He was trying to be through with that one.

Dog had filled out, what with all the sliders and chicken. Dwight called him "Fatty" a lot. He farted like an old dead man though. It would come sliding out, pffft like while they were watching TV or something and Dwight would say, "What the fuck man?" And Dog would look at him sideways while he fanned the room, swearing Dog wasn't getting any more god damn sliders. He would lick his lips and yawn, not sure what all the fuss was about.

One Sunday morning he couldn't hardly get out of bed because Dog was laid out all over everything and had him pinned down under the covers. He pushed on him and felt how solid he was. "Wake up you Fatty." Dog's head snapped up, *what?* He jumped up and stretched out his long scarred-up frame. He snorted and looked at Dwight expectantly. "No, no, you go eat some god damn dog food. I'm making pancakes, and waffles, and eggs, and bacon, and you ain't getting none of it." Dog jumped off the bed and Dwight was able to get up. Dog stamped and pranced a little, like they might go run around the house together. He let him outside and made some coffee. He sat at the kitchen table waiting for it to brew as he stared off into space, feeling dirty, and wondering when he wouldn't be doing any of this anymore. He poured coffee into the same cup he used yesterday and went outside and sat at the little picnic table on the back porch. Dog was checking all the blades of grass to see if anyone had visited the yard last night. He scouted around intently sniffing this and that, then he began to circle a particular spot. He sniffed and circled and squatted down to take a dump. Dwight watched him. He was facing slightly away from Dwight but looked over at him apologetically as he squatted down. "That's nice, real nice. I'm trying to enjoy my coffee on this peaceful morning and you decide that's a good time to take a shit. Are you upwind? Did you make sure you're upwind? That's nice. You probably didn't even need to take a shit. You saw me and thought, hell yeah, I'm gonna take me a shit." Dog looked at him forlorn, working his bowels. He finished and kicked up the grass with a happy flourish and trotted over to Dwight, *we gonna run around the house now?*

The coffee worked its magic and Dwight went in to do his own business. "You wanna come watch?" He left Dog outside to eat his dog food.

He pooped and did the rest of his bathroom stuff. He heard Dog at the back door as he came in the kitchen and saw the leash hanging next to the door as he went to let him in. Dog banged on the half-open door. "Well come on in, stupid." He got dressed and put the leash on Dog wiggling all over the place and they headed out for a walk around the neighborhood.

Dog was an easy dog to walk. He sniffed this and that, but mostly he walked a little ahead of Dwight looking around at everything; cars, squirrels, and people, ready for action if it was necessary. Dwight liked this neighborhood. It was older, and now mostly lower middle class with several older people left who had moved in when it was first built, back when it was just upper middle class. The trees were big and shady and most of the lawns were green and kept up. The younger people had cars everywhere though, some parked in the grass. Dwight always frowned when he saw a car parked up on the grass. One guy had made a dirt half-moon in his yard like a driveway in the dirt, and he had to go over the curb when he came or went. Dwight always made a point to scowl at the house when he walked by. Parking on the grass. His father would have shit a brick, he thought. Grass was for mowing, not parking on. This guy had a big jacked up yellow truck, all rutted in there, which was usually muddy. After it rained he tracked mud all over the street. *Idiot.* The younger crowd usually had 2 or 3 cars parked at crowded angles trying to fit on the driveway, half hanging out in the grass, and then 1 or 2 more taking up curb space. There were hardly any bikes in the yards though. He rarely saw kids in the street, even on the weekends. In the afternoons and weekends, the street he grew up on looked like a fair run by kids. Bikes and footballs and skateboards laying all over the place, homemade ramps, and chalk colored all over everything. From above, it probably looked like a kicked-up ant bed. Then someone would yell "Car!" and everyone would scatter to the safety of the grass, with the older, bolder ones hanging out on the fringes of the street, or trying to complete a pass over the moving car.

He walked slowly behind Dog, who every now and then, tried to make him go faster. "How the fuck are they gonna run the country if they aren't ever climbing any fucking trees?" he asked Dog. "Fat little fucks are all gonna need carpal tunnel surgery before they're thirty."

A little breeze kept the air cool, and he zoned out as Dog pulled him along. They usually made the same circuit when they walked the neighborhood, right out of the house to the first intersection, Walker Lane, then left on Walker 4 blocks to the Kwickie Mart, then left on La Salle a block, and left again onto College for 4 more blocks, and then left onto his street, Heritage. Dog would've probably walked around the whole town, but fifteen minutes walking was all the exercise Dwight needed. Dog could chase his tail in the backyard.

Dwight kept his mind blank. There was nothing he cared to think about. He used to think about all kinds of things when he laid brick. It wasn't mind-numbing work, but he didn't have to focus on it too much. He was a craftsman in a craftsman's trade, and they all knew who did what part of the wall. If the brick was slightly angled out, or the spacing was a sixteen of an inch off, or you put too many of the same bricks from the same batch in one area and from across the street it looked like a stain on the wall, you would hear about it. The homeowner might not be able to tell, but they all knew who had messed up what part. He cared about his work, and all his bricks lined up, but after years on the job, it wasn't hard. He would think about how to do the house remodel, lay plans for his next maneuvers on World War III, or how he could talk Marlene into trying some stuff she was hesitant to try. His job had been good, not great, but good. She had the insurance from her job; he made most of the money, and it worked out okay. For awhile.

He just killed time now, as there was nothing to think about. Just plod, plod along, while Dog looked at everything. He figured this was good for himself too. Good how, he didn't know, getting fresh air or something. He was liberated in his life now, though. Nothing really needed to be good for him. It didn't matter now.

He came to when he realized Dog was stopped. He was standing still, looking down a side street, his ears up. Dwight looked around. They were on College now, two blocks away from where they would take a left to go onto his street, Heritage. He looked at the street sign for this side street. Del Campo. He had never really noticed this street before. It seemed to be only a block long and stopped in a tangle of trees and bushes at a dead end. It was a long block though, almost two blocks long but without side streets. On the right was the back side of some business or vacant lots. On the left, it was hard to tell how many houses there were because they were set so far back off the street, and the whole block was crowded with big, low-hanging trees and heavy bushes. The street looked lost. Really, he could only make out one house and he could tell it was abandoned, as the front door and the front windows were covered with old plywood. He thought he could see an ancient mobile home tucked in the growth beyond that house, old and grey, but with the brown end of an old Cadillac or Buick sticking out from the side. It was lived in, he thought, maybe. Probably an old man who never went anywhere much, but there was a path from the drive to the house. And on further down, where Dog was looking, he could make out a yellow house, nearly covered in ivy or some other vine. It sat still looking quiet like a stagnant pond. Dog stared down the street, head tilted.

There was a sound on the breeze, and Dog took a few steps forward, and Dwight followed. The sound was something from the general direction of the yellow house, but it was vacant in identifiers. It was just a sound. And then the breeze brought to Dwight the smell, in a flourish of wind and leaf rattle. Just a faint bit, flicked at his nose and then gone. He stopped and breathed in deeply, searching. Nothing. He could yank on the leash and head on home and be there in five minutes, watch TV, get food, and not take walks in the neighborhood anymore. He looked down the long street, uncertain. After a moment he realized he could just see the front end of a car backed into the drive of the yellow viney house. It was small and yellow. Small and yellow.

He dropped the leash. If he'd been asked later about dropping the leash, he would not have known what to say, as to why he dropped it. Dog was his own dog, he guessed, not really his. He smelled the smell, and he headed after it. He walked quickly down the street, before nerve, or circumstance, or whatever, could stop him. He passed the mobile home, but didn't notice that the next house was also a mobile home, vacant, and drowning in vegetation. He was hurrying now, hurrying to see the yellow Festiva. The car came into view and he knew it was the same car that he followed out of the parking lot at work, and he knew this was where the big man lived, reeking in the smell, and he began to smell it more now, hanging about, mingling in the breeze. As he approached the house, he realized he was past the line, past the line of planning, of making a plan. He had none. He had nothing in his hand. He had just gotten the cast off of his right hand Tuesday, and he had nothing in either hand. No plan and nothing in his hands. He looked about the yard as he quickly approached the front door and saw what looked like old clothes in a cardboard box against the side of the house, crumpling under the weather. There seemed to be a transmission laying under the carport sticking out from behind the car. There were tires and trash around but nothing good, and then he was at the front door. He looked down at his feet and saw some sort of metal bracket to hold on a car bumper or something and he bent down and picked it up. It was a little light but one end was twisted and jagged. He pulled on the screen door quietly and put his hand on the knob, pausing. Was this it? Did it all end here? He had no idea who or how many were on the other side of the door. He knew it was the right door, as the smell leaked out from everywhere, like a gas, nauseating and beginning to choke. He paused and found a small moment where he could turn. He could let the screen door close and quietly walk away.

He could make a bit of a plan, buy a gun or something, at least get a knife. Write a letter and put in the mailbox about this house, and all the rest, in case it stopped here, for him. Then there was a bit of a yelp from inside, from a child. His body went cold, and he sighed. He turned the knob and it turned silently, come on in friend, do it. You won't. He helped the screen door close slowly behind him, leaving Dog outside.

He entered into a dark room, a dark house. There was noise from people talking, a man or maybe two men, and a child, weak and terrible. He shut the door slowly and stood to the left waiting, listening, trying to make out his surroundings. The child was being taught something. There was loud reprimand, then soft coercement, then stuttered words and crying. A slap of something on skin and Dwight stepped into the living room holding the metal piece, stunned. The room was lit only by the big TV on the wall, and on it was a movie. In front of him was a long sectional couch, with another big chair to the left. On the TV was a young boy, dirty and naked except for dirty white underwear. He was blindfolded with his hands at his side and his head down. Next to him was a man, large and fat, and wearing black pants and combat boots, but no shirt, and in his hands he had a short whip with many lashes. Dwight was frozen as he processed the scene on the TV. It was not a movie, not a real one. It was real life, a home movie.

He heard a sound to his left and saw movement but too late, as he stood mesmerized by the scene on the TV. He turned and saw a large man coming up out of his chair towards him. He had no shirt on and wore black pants and was barefoot. He was lunging at Dwight, and Dwight heard a big dog bark from the other room, loud and alarmed, and then another. *Oh shit.* The man was yelling and he had his hands raised, holding something metal in one of them, and suddenly he was there, in front of Dwight, thrusting a knife into his throat. He blocked quickly, dropping the metal piece and fell back as the knife punctured the side of his neck, and he was pushed back into a wall, and the dogs were on him, and he thought briefly, *where is Dog?* He felt the knife rupture his skin, tear through his muscle, throughout his body like electricity, down to his toes. The dogs were at his legs, biting and barking, trying to get at him around their master. The knife stabbed and ripped its way deep into his neck and he was pinned against the wall, the man with both hands on the knife, the dogs tearing at his legs. He held his hands tightly over the man's hands as he tried to stab the knife in further, grinning crazily as Dwight was trying to kick the dogs off. He looked into his eyes, and Dwight knew the man was going to kill him. His eyes were black in the darkness of the room, full of fear and anger and crazy. Dwight must have looked like a skewered rabbit, and the man began to smile around the edges of his face, and his eyes began to shine in triumph. "GET HIM!" he shouted to the dogs, and they went rabid. Dwight screamed as one of them locked onto the back of his thigh and began to shake and pull. The other one barked a constant booming bark in between snapping at any part of Dwight he could reach. "HA!" the man laughed in Dwight's face, hitting his face with spit and rotten breath. Dwight buckled against the wall, beginning to slide down.

Dog exploded into the room bowling into both dogs. The dogs left Dwight and immediately turned on Dog in a fury of barking and growling. The big man relaxed his pressure on Dwight as he backed up slightly to look beneath him to see what was happening. Dwight let go of his hands and struck him hard in the ribs, three, four times. He grunted loudly and backed off, letting go of the knife, and as he stumbled back, Dwight brought up a fist under his chin and rocked his head back. The man turned and tumbled heavily into and down the wall, crashing onto the floor.

Dwight started after him, and realized suddenly the knife was still in his neck. He swooned with dizziness, putting his hand against the wall. Before he could stop to think about it, he reached up quickly and yanked the knife out with a gasping yell. He felt his own blood run down his neck, warm under his shirt, down his chest. He slid down on one knee as the man was getting to his feet. He had to get him now. Dwight gripped the knife and jumped on top of him, stabbing it deep into the side of his thigh. He yelled tremendously and fell onto the floor again. The dogs were tearing and growling in a heap near the TV. Dwight rose up and pulled the knife out as he did. He dove on him, bringing the knife down with all he had, stabbing it into the back of his neck. He rolled violently but Dwight held him partially pinned face down. He pulled the knife out and stabbed him again under the side of his jaw. Blood was all over the handle, running down his arm, spilling over his neck. He stabbed him again and again, and again. Spent and dizzy, he lay over the moaning man, gasping. The sound of the dogs came to him from off in another room now, slowed down some but still vicious and cutting with painful yelping.

He struggled up off him and stumbled into the room with the dogs and turned on the light. Dog was backed into a corner, an ear dangling from his head, and holding one paw off the ground. His back leg was smeared with blood and a wound had skin hanging open. His mouth was torn and covered in blood. One dog was face to face with him, about to lunge, and the other was down low, trying to come in from the side. They were both cut and bloodied and the low dog looked almost done, but he was waiting for a chance to get in underneath.

The rage in Dwight was nearly beyond control. He was so mad his vision blurred and he had to focus to kick the nearest dog. He kicked him so hard he felt something pop in his knee and he went to the ground as the dog hit the wall and fell with a yelp to the floor. The fight went right out of the other dog and he made for the door. Enraged that it might get away, Dwight lunged as it went by, missing and grabbing only the edges of his back leg, and hitting his chin on the wood floor. His teeth rattled against each other and his head popped off the floor. He rolled over slowly, numb with the shock of the blow. His head spun. He found a shirt next to his hand and he brought it up to his neck, and his heart fluttered as he smeared the thick wetness against his skin. The other dog was limply crawling out of the room. He let it go.

He lay still long enough, gasping, he might have fallen asleep but for Dog's whining. He rolled onto his side and opened one eye to have a look. His heart stuttered. Dog was lying on his belly looking very hurt. Blood dripped quickly off his chin, from his ear and mouth. Dwight got up as quickly as he could, the shirt falling to the floor. There was clothing all over the floor, all over a desk and small bed, and he grabbed something and pressed it gently into the large bleeding gash in Dog's back leg. Dog winced some, but not enough. Dwight began to panic a little. He was a long four blocks from home, in the middle of the day. He was dizzy and bleeding and knew his knee was hurt. He didn't know how bad Dog was, but he wasn't trying to move. He pulled the shirt back; it was wet with blood, and the wound was nasty and torn, still bleeding a little. He found a sock and balled it up, then set it on top of the wound. He wound another shirt up and tied it firmly around the leg, pressing the sock into the wound a little. He grabbed something else and wiped at his mouth and face. "What the fuck huh? You couldn't whip two dog's asses, you little baby?" His heard the tremor in his voice. He found a bad cut on his lip, but it wasn't bleeding. The rest was just punctures and small cuts. Dog licked his lips once and whined, looking up at Dwight. "Roll over huh, ok? Yeah, easy, it's ok boy. You did fucking good." Tears were running down his face. "Oh god damn." His throat was mangled and wet, skin hanging open and dripping. Dwight decided he couldn't inspect that any further and hope to get out of this house with his dog. He found a large shirt and wound it up, tying it tight Dog's neck like a collar. "That's it bud, that's all we're gonna do right now, okay?" He bent down to pick him up and felt a bead of wetness roll down his sternum. He looked down and saw his shirt dark and red. He took it off and stuffed it in his pants. He rooted around the pile of clothes for something that wasn't too nasty and found a large red shirt. God damn, he needed a scarf, but he doubted these were scarf kind of people. *We have to get the fuck out of this house.* He found a large winter sock and tied it around his neck, covering the wound, then he put the red shirt on. He found another shirt and rolled it up, put it around his neck and stuffed the ends into the front of the shirt. He was sure he looked like a mad man, but it might do for four blocks.

He looked around, trying to think. He left Dog on the floor and went limping through the house. The man was still laying on the floor, hadn't moved, and seemed to be dead. The TV still played the home movie and he started involuntarily at the sight and sound. He forced himself to block it out as much as he could but he didn't turn it off. He wanted it to be playing when the police got there. They needed to come soon, but he need to get out first. He stepped over the man and went into the kitchen. Pans with old food were on the stove and in the sink. There was dog feces in a corner by the back door. The back door was open and the screen on the storm door was torn. Dog. His heart cinched up. There didn't seem to be a land line in the house. He went back into the living room and noticed the man's cell phone on the coffee table by his chair. The screen was lit up, and there was an app running, a game or something. There was a box of tissue and bottle of lotion on the table also. Dwight's stomach turned as he saw this as he still tried to block out the TV. He picked up the phone with a tissue and pushed the home button. The home screen popped up with a bunch of apps, and at the bottom he saw the phone icon. He put the phone in the front pocket of the shirt and went to the bathroom. The was blood spattered on his cheek some, and his eyes were red, but he didn't look too bad. He washed his hands and face and wiped off the faucet and counter with a rag.

He went to get Dog, who was laying with his head down. He bent down and picked him up quickly. Dog winced and his head spun, and they leaned precariously into the wall. Dwight panted against the wall for a moment until he felt alright to move. He moved around the furniture, limping, and he wrangled Dog through the front door, wiping the door knob with the rag as they left, half holding and half leaning Dog up against door frame, who yelped loudly in his ear. He left the door open, but the storm door slammed loudly behind them. He carried Dog under his legs, up by his own chest, panting already. Four blocks. His knee was starting to hurt. He didn't know if he could make it. He felt weak and tired. Dog looked back at him. *You can set me down,* he seemed to say. Tears threatened to flow again and he said, "Stop lookin' at me. I'll make it, we'll make it."

He huffed and limped his way to the end of the block, shielded by the backs of business on one side and trees and still houses on the other. He stopped near the stop sign at the corner of College street and walked up into a large bush and set Dog down, who yelped loudly again. He shooshed him and apologized and got the cell phone out. He dialed 911. When they answered, he told them there was a dead pedophile at the shitty yellow house at the end of Del Campo street. He told them to watch the video on the TV, and he hit the end button. He wiped the phone down and threw it as far as he could down the street into some trees and bushes. He got down on one knee and scooped Dog up as gently as he could without falling over, and headed quickly home.

Sunday morning and people seemed to be everywhere. A lady was jogging south as he headed north, but she was across the street. He walked straight down the sidewalk, trying to prepare something to say when she noticed him and his bloody dog. People wouldn't say anything to you by yourself, but have a dog with you and its social hour on the sidewalk. She never even turned, never slowed. From the glance out of the corner of his eye, he thought she probably got looked at a lot when she jogged and she probably made it a practice to ignore passing men.

Two blocks left and he met the first car. Everyone in the car eyeballed him as he walked by, and he could see them talking. He tried to nod his head like, *yeah, got into a dog fight, but he's fine.* They slowed but he kept walking and they finally went on. On Heritage street now. One of his old neighbors was out hand watering his whole lawn, trees, flowers, grass, everything, like he did all summer. Dwight was almost passed before he raised his head and notice.

"Hey, hey! What happened? Are you alright? Hey!"

Dwight didn't stop and didn't even slow. He was nearly done. He couldn't feel his arms and Dog had started to shift uncomfortably as he slid further down Dwight's chest, and was hanging down by his belt now. He couldn't stop. "Dog fight!" he yelled over his shoulder. "My house is right there. I gotta get him to the vet," he said weakly, and kept walking.

"Do you need a ride?"

He nearly collapsed against his truck door, leaning Dog heavily into it. He just managed to raise him up some to get to the handle and open the door. He set Dog on the front seat and just laid against the seat. He finally slid down and fell on his butt, hitting his head against the open door as he rolled onto his back. He dimly listened for sounds of the old man, trying to work up a story as his head spun. He breathed rapidly, arms and legs splayed out on the ground. After a few moments, Dog whined softly. He rolled over and got on his hands and knees and looked toward the old man's house, and saw no one. *Calling the cops probably.* He got up slowly and limped into the house and got his keys. He climbed into the front seat and started the truck. Then he pulled out his cell phone and called a number he hadn't called in more than a year.

"Hello," she said flatly after the 6th ring. There was everything in that one word. I hate you, why are you calling, you're probably drunk, are you okay, what do you want, I'm trying to live again so leave me alone!

"I need you now." He paused and she said nothing. "I'm hurt bad, I think, and so is this dog, and I need your help. I can't go to the hospital or the vet. Will you look at my dog? Please?" And suddenly he found he was crying, soft blubbering, ugly and strained, like only men can do.

"I'm at work!" she said. "Why are you hurt? What happened? Are you crying? You don't have a dog. Why can't you go to the hospital, or the vet? What happened?"

161

He collected himself enough to say, "I don't want to bother you…but I need help now…I don't know what else to do. Will you look at the dog, please? Now? Maybe bring some stuff for stitches. Can you meet me at your house? I can't wait for you to drive all the way over here. He's not home is he?"

"What is wrong?"

He didn't know what to say so he said the main facts. "Knife wound in my neck and the dog was torn up by two other dogs, he's got at least two bad tears in him and he's bleeding a lot. And his ear is torn off." He waited.

"Oh my god," she said softly, unbelieving. "I'm leaving now. He's not home." She hung up.

He looked over at Dog, who lay still with his head on the seat. He touched him softly above his tail. "You okay?" He whined and kept his head down. Dwight could see blood smeared on his faded green seat. He backed out and headed to Marlene's.

She lived about 10 minutes away, on the north side. He'd driven by a couple times after they'd first moved there, in moments of depression, but he'd never stopped, never been inside. He drove with the noon Sunday traffic, in a daze, lightheaded and sad. Surely, he must be near the end. He wondered what would happen to Dog. Maybe Marlene would take him. He thought not. He thought briefly about his old friends and found no one. *Hey, this is Dwight, yeah you remember my daughter was abducted and killed, naw I'm good, well anyway, I know we haven't talked, you know, because you haven't called to check on me because it was too uncomfortable and much easier just to let it go, and I haven't called you because I'm dead inside, but would you take my dog?*

A loud HONK blasted from the car behind him, and he almost put it in park to get out and beat the shit out of someone, he had his left hand already on the door handle and his right positioned to put the truck in park, but he was too weak. He needed to get Dog looked at. He didn't even look in the rearview mirror, but he felt a rush of blood through his system, and it woke him up. He let his foot off the brake and pulled through the green light.

He pulled up to the curb in front of her nice, suburban home, bricked in the front, but siding all around the rest of the house. This was part of letting him go. He hated these fake front brick houses. She knew it too. It was like makeup for houses, he said. I'm not really durable and strong, it's just for pretend. He hated her boyfriend even more when he saw his home. *Poser.*

But he didn't care now. He really only had one thing on his mind just now, Dog. He didn't have the room, or the give a shit for anything else. He was tired. He lived like he was dead, with only brief moments of being alive at The Shame. The smell had been keeping him going. Without it, there was nothing for him, and he wanted there to be nothing. But he would get this dog fixed. This dog deserved something good, and he deserved a good home. He knew Marlene would take good care of him; he didn't know about her boyfriend. He probably liked cats.

She pulled up into her drive like she owned the place, coming to a rocking stop. She was a little bigger, but she looked good. Her hair was done up in a casual but sort of young-ish way, pinned on one side and pulled back with another pin on the other. He got out and put his foot slightly angled on the curb, felt his knee give, and fell onto the grass of her yard. His neck throbbed as he landed palms down, and he swayed there for a second. His eyes opened a few moments later and focused on her little nurses shoes in the grass by his hands, light blue trimmed in pink, and her pink scrub bottoms. She said nothing. He pulled himself up by the door not looking at her, and moved his hand along the edge of the truck guiding his way around to the other side. He opened the door and held it back for her to look inside. Then he looked at her face as she came around, his wife, Abigail's mother, the woman from his real life, and he felt it rushing at him, the sadness. This living, breathing, innocent and beautiful reminder of what he had done, what he used to have, who he used to be, and what he no longer had. Before she got to Dog it crushed him, and he crumpled on the street, down on his knees and head in his hands, crying and bawling. Ashamed but unable to stop, he cried and cried. He didn't feel her at first, but finally her warmth and her smell was next to him, and she hugged over the top of him and cried with him. She held onto him like a part of her had always wanted to, and for a moment she did hold on, and they finally mourned her together.

He didn't know how long they sat there, but he finally recovered and wiped his face on the nasty red shirt and was instantly reminded of Dog. She felt him stir and she straightened up, wiping her face unsuccessfully with her hands and sleeve. "God, your shirt stinks."

Before she could ask anything, he said, "He needs to go to the vet. Will you take him? If you have a trash bag or plastic, I'll put him in the back of your car?"

She looked at him before she looked at the dog. He had someone else's shirt on, as that dirty thing was big enough for two Dwight's, and he had a sock, which had blood on it, tied around his neck. He also had a shirt over his neck, tucked into the front of the red shirt. His jeans were torn and bloody, and it looked like both he and the dog had been in a fight with dogs. She wanted to ask why he couldn't take his dog to the vet, but she knew it was a waste of time. He was wounded on the neck, stabbed he said. He was pale and gaunt. And he had a full beard. Well he would. She said it poked her lips when they kissed and she would never let him grow one. She looked in at the dog. He was a boxer of some sort, greyish and brown though. He was not in the mood to move and only looked up at her. There was blood smeared underneath him. He was hurt pretty bad. She turned and went to her car and opened the garage door. She went in and came back out with a little floor matt. Dwight saw her open the back hatch on her SUV and he went in and picked up Dog. He whined again and Dwight told him to quit milking it. He laid him on top of the rug and she hit the button to shut the door.

She got in her car, started it, and rolled down the window. "Stay here," she said. "I'll be back in 25 minutes."

He hesitated, and she waited for him to do his man thing.

"Just tell them he's your neighbor's dog and…"

"I'm gonna tell them I found him on the side of the road. Don't you fucking leave." And she drove off.

He stepped back and watched her leave. A part of him relaxed, a big part really, most of what he had left. He limped over to his truck and got in before he fell down. He lay down in the seat over Dog's blood and closed his eyes.

Forty-five minutes later, she stood at his truck looking at him sleeping through the dirty window. She could just see the tear in the jeans on the back of his thigh. A small patch of blood stain on the jeans below the tear, puffy and bruised skin with puncture marks. She walked around to the passenger side. He was still wearing the ugly red shirt and the other shirt was still wrapped around his neck and partially tucked in. His hat was askew against the seat and his hair was long and uncut, and unwashed. His face was covered in beard, but calm.

"What have you been doing?" she said softly. She tapped on the window with her keys and he jerked up immediately. His face grimaced and his hands went to his neck. She watched his eyes focus and she tapped gently on the glass again, waved for him to follow and walked in front of the truck toward the house. She heard his door creak open slowly and heard him grunt. She went inside, leaving the front door open.

Stars popped all around his vision as he slid out of the truck. He sat there a few seconds with his butt against the seat and his feet on the ground, his hand on the open door. She was back so Dog should be getting worked on. He pushed off from the truck and shut the door, swaying slightly. He staggered slowly across the lawn.

"In here!" she yelled from down a hallway as he entered the house. He tried not to look at anything in her house. He followed the sound which led through the master bedroom, into the master bathroom. He winced as he crossed through the master bedroom, bed unmade, clothes here and there, lived in. He winced again at the amount of light as he entered the bathroom. She was by the sink counter, leaning on it with one hand, waiting. She pointed to the toilet for him to sit. "This room has the most light. Take that nasty shit off."

He looked around lost for a moment, then pulled off the shirt wrapped around his neck. He held on to it as he tried to wriggle out of the big red shirt, his neck pulsing and throbbing.

"Wait, wait," she said. She grabbed the shirt out of his hand and threw it into the trash, then she grabbed her scissors and began to cut the red shirt off. He stood mutely, arms out slightly. "God that stinks," she said as she threw it into the trash also.

"Burn it," he said. "Burn it all."

She stopped and looked at him. Then she gestured with the scissors to the toilet. He sat down on the closed seat. "What happened?"

He didn't know what to say or where to begin. His mind was spent and he was tired. She watched him stare off into space and fear crept up on her. She fully expected this to be a bar fight and somehow dogs were involved, or at the outside, he was into dog fighting and it got out of hand. He looked so tired, so lost, and so sad. Her heart began to get hot, but she shut it down. *I will not feel something for him!*

She bent down and began cutting the sock off his neck. She pulled it off and gasped inside. It was vertical stab wound longer than an inch on the front right side of his neck, swollen and red, matted and smeared with blood all around the edges. She dropped the sock into the trash. "You need to go to the hospital."

He still didn't say anything. His head dropped a little. "Can you put some stitches in it?"

She barked at him, "Why the fuck can't you go to the hospital?"

He sighed. "I can I guess, it probably doesn't matter much. Do they call the cops when you come in with a stab wound?"

She sighed. "What did you do? Oh my god, let me look at it."

He sat silent while she mulled over it, gently prodding. "I brought a local. I can give you that and put some stitches in, I guess. Shit."

"When will he be home?"

She stiffened. "He's playing golf."

"Ok," he gave a nod and slight crinkle to the edge of his mouth.

"You ready?" She held up the needle. He nodded. She wanted to jab it into his brain, but instead she put it softly into his neck and injected the anesthetic. She began to clean the wound, and the area around it.

"Did you get the dog in okay?"

"Yeah, I probably lost my vet though. They all kept giving me looks like I was into dog fighting or something. He's okay. A nasty tear under his throat, but just skin mostly. The bite on his leg is bad, but it'll heal okay. He's a good dog."

His face tightened, and she realized he was trying not to cry again. She waited patiently. Finally, he said softly, "I got him at the first one." She readied the needle and was starting on the stitches when that finally registered and she straightened up. "The first one what?"

"I…" He really didn't know what to say.

She couldn't take much more of this. "If you've done something illegal, I'll just deny you said anything to me. You came over with the dog and I took him to the vet and stitched up a knife wound. You're taking those clothes with you. You got into a fight? What did you do, you kill him?" She didn't believe that but she had to get him started.

He nodded his head slowly. "Yeah. Him and three others. Four."

He braced for her to yell at him and kick him out, phone in hand. But really, he knew she wouldn't do that. She straightened up. "Four what? People?" He confirmed it by saying nothing. She struggled to understand what he was trying to tell her. "Why?"

He paused one more time, before he made everything even worse for her with what he was about to say. Then he said, "You remember at her funeral, when I, I picked her up?"

The bathroom went very quiet. He was aware of the scissors gripped tightly in her hand by his neck. Her face was quivering, "Yesss."

"I'm sorry."

He was apologizing for everything. She was near to bursting now, so he hurried on.

"Something happened. And you can just listen to me and not believe it. I don't care. I don't understand it, but she passed something to me, or something was passed to me, I don't know. There was an awful smell coming off her, not her, not her death, but something wretched, like sewer and rot and wrongness, and...it was overwhelming. It was transferred to me. It wasn't her, but it came off of her. I think it was because of what was done to her. It's a smell, and I can smell it on other people, people who do those kinds of things to kids. It led me to five of them. And I killed four of them."

"What?" she said softly. He looked up at her and held her eyes calmly. He wasn't going to force this on her; he didn't even know what was going on, but he did believe in it. He was going to follow this smell until he was dead. He had no other plans.

"You've killed four people you think were...because you could smell it on them?"

"Did you hear about the guy who owned the daycare, who was molesting the kids there for fifteen years? He got stabbed in his home...The guy killed in his bathroom over by the bar The Shame? I don't know if it came out what he was doing or not. The choir instructor at Oakville Baptist Church? It might not come out what he was doing either. Then this guy, today..." He stopped, his head hanging. "He was bad. He made films with kids. I walked into his house and there he was, watching one of them on TV. He had two dogs in the house, and I just walked in with nothing...Dog saved me." He had his hands in his lap, his eyes staring into the shower curtain.

"You can smell them?" was all she could say.

"WHAT THE FUCK DWIGHT! You've killed four fucking people because you *think* they're molesting children? You can *smell* them doing it? Oh my fucking god. You think you can fix it? You think you can fix it? You can NEVER fix what happened to her! She is GONE, broken,…murdered…" she faded into sobs, standing there with her hands to her face, scissors in one and a needle in the other. "You should…have been watching her…now you're killing people you don't even know they've done anything…"

"I'm almost done, Marlene. I'd be done already if it weren't for that dog. It can't last much longer. Those four motherfuckers I killed, will *no longer* hurt little children. I *know* what they were doing. I *don't* know what happened between me and Abigail, but I can smell them like I can smell your perfume, except it's stronger, much stronger, like an open sewer or a pile of rotting flesh, and I can hardly stand it sometimes. But it leads me straight to 'em, and I fucking kill them. I don't know what's going on, and I don't really give a shit. I'm not making up for Abigail…I am dead from that…I will never recover. She's was taken and abused and killed and I was TWENTY FEET AWAY…PLAYING FUCKING VIDEO GAMES!" He spluttered out, crying, snot running out his nose and blood trickling from his neck. "I'm not looking for your approval." He tried to reach around for some toilet paper but flinched when he turned his head. She reached down and got him a wad, then pulled some off for herself.

He blew his nose and wiped off his face. "I've got this now. It's real. I don't care what it is or where it comes from. If it comes from the devil, all I can say is what took you so fucking long?"

Her hands shook as she dropped her toilet paper into the trash. She daubed off his neck a little longer than necessary, but she was trying to steady her hands. They were both quiet while she finished stitching him up. She put a bandage over the wound and sat down on the side of the tub. He looked at her.

"They had it coming. They're not doing that anymore. This one…" he brought a hand up to his neck but stopped short of touching it, "…was very bad."

She wanted to say something, but all of it seemed wrong.

He wanted to ask her if he was good to her, but it wouldn't go well. She would bristle up. All he could think of was, "You look good." She did, she seemed okay, she was recovering, but he instantly regretted saying it.

She bowed her head and cried again. He reached back without looking and pulled off some paper and put it in her hands. "God damn it…" she mumbled. "I *was* doing good. Thanks for dropping all this on me. I miss her…I miss my family. Sometimes I think I'm just lying, it's all just a big fucking lie. He wants kids…I don't know if I can do it…"

He leaned over and put a hand on her knee, "Kids need good moms. Okay?"

She blew her nose, and he pulled back. She finished and said, "You really can smell them? How does that work?"

He shrugged. "They reek. You ever walk by one of those old ladies who douse themselves in perfume and they go by you in like a cloud, and you can't breathe for a minute? It's like that, except it makes me want to puke, does make me puke. So, I follow them and I see what they're doing. It becomes obvious when you look. I make sure."

"Why Dwight? If you know, why do you kill them? Just turn over the information to the police. You're gonna go to jail, or get killed." She motioned to his neck.

"The first one," he paused, "I caught in the act, and I was so furious, thinking about her. I couldn't stop. And then, I didn't want them to go to jail. I wanted them to die. I want to kill them all. With some good lawyers and some sketchy evidence, they might not even go to jail. Then shit, when they get in jail, they'll find jesus and get reformed and write children's books and go on talk shows. No, fuck that. I'm just gonna do this."

"When you grabbed her, you smelled it?"

He looked at her and nodded. They sat silent for a while. She got up and grabbed some pills out of her bag. She filled a glass with water and gave it to him, "Take these."

She took the glass back and cleaned up her things. She wrapped the dirty clothes in a plastic bag and said, "Come sit at the table," as she left the bathroom. He got up slowly and looked around the bathroom. Then he made his way into the kitchen area and sat at the table, as she came in and handed him a shirt. He put it on, knowing whose it was. She walked out the back door into the back yard with the plastic bag in her hand. He watched her through the window drop the bag into a little fire pit they had just off the porch and spray lighter fluid all over it. She dropped a match on it, and then she stood there with it while it burned down, occasionally adding more fluid and poking at it with a stick.

When she came back in the kitchen she became a flurry of activity for a few minutes, and then brought two sandwiches on plates, and set one down in front of him. Before he could help himself, he said, "No chips?" as she walked back into the kitchen.

She grabbed two sodas out of the refrigerator and got a can of Pringles dill pickle flavor and banged them down on the table in front of him. She gave him his soda and sat down with hers across the table from him. He smiled to himself, but she saw him and said, "Fuck you. He likes those nasty ass chips too."

He quickly focused on his meal, not daring to think about her, or her new man, or that she had to buy him the same chips. After a few minutes she said, "What kind of knife was it, was it clean?"

A light bulb popped in his head, and he stopped mid chew. "Oh fuck," he said softly. "I left it there."

Quickly she said, "Can you go back and get it?"

"No, no they'll be crawling all over there by now." He chewed automatically. "I called them. I wanted to make sure they got there before someone else did, his partner maybe, if he had one. I didn't want anyone to clean up anything. I wanted them to walk in and see the video playing on the TV."

Then she said, "You got fingerprinted, didn't you?"

She never forgot anything. He nodded his head, "When I worked on that job at the international airport. We all had to get checked out because of all the fucking terrorists. I'm on file. I killed him with his own knife. Then I got to worrying about Dog, and everything else."

"Does he not have a goddamn name?"

He smiled sadly, thinking the cops would be there when he got home. "Dog is his name." He picked at the little pieces of chip left on his plate.
 "Do you need a dog?"
He looked up at her, asking.

"I can't. He's allergic to pet dander." Dwight scoffed before he could stop himself.

"He'll be ready to go home this afternoon. I'll bring him by." *Time to go Dwight.*

"God dammit," he said softly, talking about the knife. He got up and started for the kitchen.

"Dwight…"

He stopped, holding the plate and the coke, looking at her.

"What's your plan here?" she said angrily. "Do you have one? You just gonna kill as many as you can until you get arrested, or get killed?"

He held his hands out. "I don't know. I don't know. I'm taking this chance to put some of them down…to save some kids before it happens to them. This is my plan, this is it."

She made a tsk noise and looked away, disgusted, tearing up again.

He thought of something just then. "You remember that book you made me read? About that guy who was a loner, and couldn't get on with anybody in the world, and had kind of-"

"The Catcher in the Rye."

"-of a shit life? Yeah, The Catcher in the Rye. You remember what I thought about-"

"You said it was stupid. How dumb, you said, the only way he could be happy was to put all those little kids in danger of falling off a cliff so he could stand there while they played, and watch them, keeping them from falling off with his arms. I was so mad at you."

"Yeah, it was dumb, I thought. But that's me. I'm gonna stand there and watch them while they play, with all those twisted perverts running around loose, and I'm gonna watch them, and I will take out whoever fucks with them." He turned, stomach all knotted up, and put his plate and can on the counter. He paused as he started to head out the door. He looked at her and said, "Thank you."

"The main character was shallow and stupid Dwight, is that what you are now?"

He shrugged. "I can protect some of them, and I'm going to."

She got up slowly, struggling with herself, and walked over and hugged him briefly. He embraced her tightly for a second, feeling her hair against his face, smelling her. She parted too quickly and walked off down the hall. He looked around her home briefly and went out the front door and got in his truck and left.

About halfway home he realized he was sort of in a good mood. He felt bruised and tired, but that sandwich had been great. It had filled him right up. He thought it was the best fucking sandwich he had ever eaten. Also, those pills had started to do something and his mind floated around a little. He seemed to have been smiling for some time, and he relaxed his face and sighed soberly. He had been holding that one moment with her, when she hugged him, in his mind, replaying it, smelling her again. He could not get over the feel of her hair against his cheek and wished he didn't have a beard. He drove on auto pilot, one hand on the wheel and one in his lap, staring ahead. He still saw the sadness in her face, and he felt sad for her, but he could do nothing for that. No one could do anything for that. Time would soften the punch, but it would always be there with her, when she saw a little face, when she passed a playground, or when people talked about their children. He mulled it over for a bit and thought, fuck it, that's who she is right now. That's what she's got. She was dealing with it before he showed up, and she'll deal with it again. Or she won't.

He pulled into his drive and parked, killing the engine. He sat and leaned his head back against the seat, closing his eyes. His hands relaxed onto his lap, and he breathed out slowly. The long day swirled around in his head like clouds, some dark with lighting crackling through them, but some soft and billowing. The feel of Marlene. Dog charging in to help him, ragged and bloody, his brave dog. That fucking knife. That knife being rammed into his neck. Close to dying, so close to dying. The poor boy on the TV. That sandwich, made by someone who used to love him. Tears slowly rolled out of his eyes.

He wiped off his face with his hand and crawled out of his truck. He was always crying now it seemed. It was probably 2 or 3 in the afternoon, he didn't know. He went inside, shut the door, and took off the shirt and laid it over a chair. He went into the bathroom intending to run a bath, but stopped and looked at himself in the mirror. His hair was stiff looking and long, too long. It hung down below his ears a few inches, and hung down into his eyes in places. His beard was wild, like brambles, growing down his neck and high up on his cheeks. Part of the bandage Marlene had put on was covering some of the beard. His pale white chest was fattening at the pecs due to the fast food diet and lack of exercise. His belly was protruding on its own now. He had always been a slender man. Now he was fat and sallow. His eyes were red and bloodshot around the edges, puffy too, from all the crying.

He left his depressing image in the mirror and turned on the bath, throwing a bar of soap in it. He took off his jeans and looked at his legs. The back of his right thigh was purple and red, with several teeth marks having broken the skin, red with clear puss over them. His left shin was the same, just not as big or deep. There was a tear in the bottom of his pants where one of them had tugged on it for a while. He looked all over, but there seemed to only be the big two bites. Marlene had not looked at them, and he had not asked her to.

He went into the kitchen in just socks and got a highball glass and put some ice in it, added some water, and filled it with scotch. He went back into the bathroom and adjusted the water in the tub as he sat on the cold toilet seat. He sipped the drink while the bath filled, and then got in. He hadn't taken a bath since he was a bricklayer. Sometimes when he was on a job with scaffolding, going up and down all day in the cold, in the evening Marlene would run him a bath. She'd put aromatic oil and Epsom salt in it, light candles, and fix him a drink. Then she'd sit in there with him on the toilet and chat about her day while he soaked. Sometimes he didn't want her in there while he relaxed, didn't want to hear about her day at nursing school and didn't want to know how her rounds went during her on the job training. He liked to hear her talk, but he didn't really listen.

Some time later, he woke up because the water in the tub had gone cold and he was shivering. "Shit," he mumbled. He got out and dried off, avoiding the mirror. He wanted to shave his face but he didn't have any clippers and he didn't want to sit there all night cutting it down with scissors so he could shave the rest of it off. He needed a haircut too. He could go get his hair cut at the Snappy Cuts and then go to the Walmart and get some clippers. He sighed. It was too much and he didn't want to do it. Besides, he wanted to be here when Dog got home. He thought of the bill for the vet and went to get some cash for Marlene. He felt a rising excitement at seeing her again. He stamped it down like a bug that accidentally scurries out from under the fridge while you're standing there. He tried to anyway. It was one of those cockroaches you could smash three times with your boot heel, only to see it go limping off back under the fridge.

He got dressed and got down an old work boot from the closet. He reached in and pulled out a roll of bills, and pulled off two hundred dollar bills. Then he thought it might be more than that so he got two more. He looked at the rest. It seemed like four or five hundred more in twenties. He kept it all and put the boot back.

He looked around the sparse house. It was fairly neat, mostly because he didn't do much in it. He went to the kitchen and cleaned the dishes in the sink and put those up. It was four o'clock. He didn't know what else to do, so he sat on the couch and put the football game on. He stared at the TV, but he wasn't watching. A while later, he heard a car pull up, and then a door close. And then another door closed. His heart jumped and he realized he was nervous. He was with her.

He got up and opened the door. She was standing at the back of her car, and he was leaning into the back.

"Wait!" Dwight said too loudly. "Wait, I'll get him." He hurried over, knowing he looked foolish. He got to the back of the car and he was standing there, in khakis and a golf shirt that said something golf-ish on the chest, and wearing a hat that said some more golf stuff. The hat probably cost $50. Dwight thought his outfit said *I play golf and you don't*. Dwight kind of ignored him and looked in the car. Dog was laying in the back on a towel, his head down. He tried to raise it up, but Dwight could see it was a struggle.

"He's still doped up," Marlene said. "The vet said just put him somewhere he can sleep it off. He can walk on the leg, but it'll be sore. Don't let him do anything for a few days. You can take the stitches out yourself in two weeks, or you can take him back to the vet." She said this last part like that's not what he should do.

Dog's leg and neck were shaved. The tear on his leg was about 6 inches and curved like a half moon. The one on his neck looked a little like a U. He reached in under his body and gently picked him up, grunting under the strain. Her man started to say something helpful but he stopped, and Dwight thought Marlene might have grabbed his elbow or something. He maneuvered Dog out of the car and Marlene walked ahead of him to the door.

"Get the door please, Marlene." He said her name to discourage him from doing it. She looked back at him like *that's what I'm doing dumbass*. She was wearing loose fitting jeans, a t-shirt and a rumpled ball cap, with her ponytail hanging out the back.

He shuffled through the door sideways and brought Dog over to the couch, setting him down. Dog tried to get up, while his eyes rolled around in his head. "No, just lay down. It's alright man, lay down," he said to him softly. He pushed down on him firmly until he laid his head down on the couch, finally closing his eyes.

He looked up at Marlene. She had her husband's shirt in her hand.

How much was it?"

She got out a receipt, saying, "$375."

He handed her the whole roll of bills and said before she could count it, "I'm not going to argue about this, so please don't. There's more there than $375. I don't have any use for it, and I don't have anyone else to give it to." She hesitated, and looked at the roll, and then back at Dwight.

"I imagine they'll be here tomorrow."

"Have you heard from them?"

"No."

"Maybe they couldn't get prints off the knife. Was there anything else you left behind? Did you touch anything else?"

"I don't know, probably. I was busy. Oh...I had a piece of metal. I left that too." He watched her fidget. "No, I don't have a plan."

She brought her hand to her head, "Oh my god."

He wanted to say something to her, something she wanted to hear, but his mind was disjointed, bouncing around. He couldn't concentrate with her here. He really just wanted to hold her again. He saw the roll of money in her hand and he suddenly thought of the money in his bank account, and he wanted her to have that too. What happened to your money when you went to jail for life? It would probably go to his dumb dad, or his stupid brother, he thought. He hadn't talk to either of them since the funeral.

"Hey. Hey, I can write you a check and if they arrest me you can cash it. Cash it that day, okay?" He went started into the kitchen to get the checkbook.

"WHAT are you *talking* about?" she barked at him.

He turned and looked at her, taken aback. "I have some money in my account." As if that explained it. "If they arrest me…I can't use it in prison."

"I don't want your money," she hissed at him. "If they don't come arrest you, you'll need it, and I don't want to be fucking with you anymore!" Her face was red and hot, and her eyes were full of tears. He sobered from his little plan and turned his head from her. He took a few steps into the kitchen, turning his back. He wished she were not here anymore.

There was a long silence, and he felt he should say something but he didn't know what to say. He turned back to her and was startled to see the look on her face.

It was red and tight, gnarled up in a painful looking grimace. She walked up to him and put her hand on his arm, locking her eyes onto his. She seemed very angry and was shaking slightly.

"If they don't find you…kill them. Kill them all."

His eyes involuntarily went wide. Hers were blazing behind a shimmer of tears. She let his arm go and walked to the door. She stopped with her back to him.

"If you need me…if you call me, I will come." She said this with effort, but he knew she meant it.

He relaxed and said, "Ok." And she left.

"Holy shit," he said after the door shut. He heard her car door close, and he quickly followed and opened the front door and went outside. Their car was already backing up, and he held up his hands to the glare of the windshield, looking directly where he would be. The car stopped and Dwight motioned for him to come here. The car rocked slightly as he put it in park. He opened the door and came around the front of the car to where Dwight was standing.

Dwight held out his hand and they shook hands. Dwight said, "I've caused you a lot of trouble and I'm sorry." He looked at Dwight for a moment and said simply, "It's okay man." Dwight was glad he didn't say something like, "No problem, Chief" or "Hey man, always glad to help".

"I didn't mean to bother you today, and I won't do it again."

He nodded his head, not necessarily in agreement. He looked at Dwight's neck and said, "Did you get in any on him?"

"Oh, no not really. He ran off after he did this. I've got more mouth than fight."

"You couldn't go to the police?" A question he had undoubtedly already asked Marlene.

"Uh, no, man. It was one of those deals. I couldn't." He left it at that. "I won't bother you again." Dwight took a step back. He nodded his head slightly at Dwight, and then got back in the car.

Dwight walked back to the house as they left, thinking how uncomfortable it might be in their car right now. He had dealt with a lot already with Marlene. There must be something to him, something good for her. If he couldn't weather this little storm, now was a good time for her to find out.

He entered the house quietly and soft stepped over to the couch. Dog was knocked out, sleeping heavily. He laid a hand gently on his head and was suddenly overcome with emotion at the sight of him. He straightened up to avoid crying again. "Good fucking dog," he blurted out softly.

Dwight went into the bedroom and laid on the unmade bed. His neck throbbed and his legs hurt. His knee wasn't too bad though. He fell asleep wondering when the cops would arrive.

He heard some rustling in the living room a few hours later and got up to check on Dog, who was sitting up awkwardly on the couch. He looked at Dwight and wagged his nub, and gave a little whine.

"Hey you stupid piece of shit," Dwight said softly. "Are you still alive? You worthless dog." He sat down on the couch next to him and Dog tried to get in his lap and got in a quick lick to his face. "Oh hell no, we don't do that. You lick your ass, your balls, and your pecker with that thing. You're fucking nasty." He rubbed and petted any part of him that didn't seem damaged. His heart swelled as he looked him over. "Goddamn, they fucked you up didn't they? Did you see me kick the shit outta that one? Right into the wall, goddamn dog." Dog wiggled and endured the petting as best he could. Dwight said mean things to him but the tone was all Dog heard. "You hungry, you dumb son of a bitch? We ain't got shit to eat, but let's go check. Can you walk?" Dwight got up off the couch and waited to see if he could get down. Dog got down off the couch easily enough but winced when his back leg hit. He stood there for a second trying to figure out what was wrong with it, as if he hadn't just gotten into a fight with two dogs. He limped on it experimentally, then decided it was okay, and hobbled into the kitchen, letting Dwight know he hadn't forgotten about the food talk.

"There ain't shit in here, man. I told you. You better hope there's some spam or some shit, 'cause I ain't going to the store." He rooted around through the stuff he had just bought at the store. He had a bag of dog food for him but that wouldn't do. "Well look at this you lucky little fucker, some goddamn tuna. You ain't never had no goddamn tuna. You're gonna love this shit, like caviar for dogs."

He scooped the tuna out onto a plate. It didn't look like much. Dog looked up at him. "Hmmm, what else we got…? Oh, shit ya, French bread." He picked up the loaf and put two pieces on the plate then put another can of tuna on top of it, letting the juice soak into the bread. "This is more than you deserve. Can't even beat two dog's asses at one time, you big baby. Good thing I showed up."

He set the plate down and Dog went at it tentatively. "You don't know about French bread, so shut the fuck up. You lick your butt. You'll be alright." Dog was steady eating the tuna surprise. Dwight filled a glass with water and poured it in his water bowl. He watched him eat. Dog finished up and Dwight knelt down beside him and hugged him gently around the neck. "You good little mother fucker," he said, scratching and petting.

The next day Dwight woke up around eleven. Dog was rooting around in his own crotch area, looking like he was trying to find something, slurping and licking. "It sounds like two walruses making out in here." Dog ignored him and continued working. Dwight got up and felt the pain in his leg bites, and his knee was still sore. He limped in to use the bathroom and he managed to catch himself in the mirror again. "Ok, I gotta get this shit fixed," he said looking at the hair all over his head. He had washed it in the bath the yesterday, so he figured there wouldn't be too much in it for the barber to notice.

He got dressed and said to Dog, "C'mon, big dummy."

He and Dog limped out of the house like a scene on the movie Reservoir Dogs. He reached down and helped Dog into the truck and said, "Oh goddamn," when he saw the blood still on the seat. Dwight went back into the house and looked for some cleaner. He came back out with a bottle of Windex and a rag. He scooched Dog over to the driver side saying, "Move over stupid." He cleaned it up and threw the towel in the shed trash can, leaving the Windex in there also.

He opened the driver side truck door to find Dog still sitting there. "Well move back over, dang." Dog looked at him like *Really man?* and finally moved over and laid down on the seat gingerly. "You still hurt, huh? Yeah, it'll be awhile."

He drove to White Castle and went through the drive through. Dwight ordered eight double bacon cheeseburger sliders, but four without onions, and a Mr. Pibb. The onions made Dog fart something gross, like air made of feces. Dwight could almost feel the poop particles in the air, landing on his face. He pulled around to a parking spot in the shade and they ate their feast. He had five and Dog had three, since he'd already had breakfast. It was Monday morning and Dwight hadn't bothered to call in to work. He supposed he should. He got out his phone and saw that he hadn't missed any calls. *Fuck it.* If they didn't care, he didn't care.

Dwight thought about what he should do as he chewed on the soggy burger. He knew in his heart he had left fingerprints on that knife, probably that piece of metal too. They would come get him soon. He dropped his job off his list of things to worry about. He was done working. He looked over at Dog, who was watching him eat his last burger. He, of course, was already done. "Fuck you, Dog." Dog looked at him like *ain't we friends?*

"Who can I find to take you? You're ugly, you stink, and you're nearly broken." Dog licked his lips, *go get me some more.*

He looked over his checkbook last night, and was surprised to see he had about six thousand in there. He wanted to give it to Marlene, but he knew that was wrong. She was best left alone. Before

Abigail had been killed, he had hardly talked with his dad and brother, and now he never cared to talk with them again. During the funeral, his brother and dad had been off to the side talking, like they usually were, and Dwight thought he heard his brother say something about "parenting". They always paired off against him, even when they were kids. His father always seemed disappointed in him for some reason, but he loved his little brother. Dwight had been a little rough on his younger brother when they were kids, but he was trying to make him tough. His brother was always running inside and tattling and their dad would come outside and yell at him. They had never gotten along well.

When he heard, or thought he heard, the comment from his brother at the funeral, he became enraged. In his grief and guilt, what Dwight heard him say was this wouldn't have happened if Dwight had been watching her. He might not have said that, but that's what it seemed like to him. His head snapped around and he got up from his seat intent on hurting his brother, but they stopped him, his father yelled at him, and there had been a scene. His father kept standing near his brother in a protective way as Dwight was calmed down. Dwight had noticed. He hadn't heard from them since. *No, fuck them.*

He finished his meal and started the truck. He had to get this scraggly hair cut off of his head and face. He went to the old part of downtown and parked in front of the barber shop. He rolled the windows down some and told Dog, who had his head down on the seat, to not go anywhere. Inside the barber shop there was one old man getting his sparse hair trimmed up for probably the second time this month, by the ancient owner of the shop, Ed, and another old man waiting in a chair for Ed to finish. The other chair with a younger barber, was empty. The young barber looked up as Dwight entered and motioned to Dwight that his chair was empty. Dwight didn't even bother asking the other old man if he was next in line. He sat down as the young man greeted him.

"How's it going man?"

"Good man, how are you?"

"Golden brother. Dang, has it been awhile?" He said agreeably as Dwight took off his hat.

"Yeah. I try and stay ugly so the chicks don't bother me too much."

The young barber laughed. "Right? I wish I had that problem. I try to stay pretty, but it just ain't working."

"Yeah, it's a curse."

"I bet. Wow, what happened? One of them bite you?"

"No, she stabbed me."

He laughed again. "Dang. Okay, what are we doing today man? You want me to braid it? Maybe put some highlights in it?"

"Shave it all off, man."

"All of it?"

"Yeah, like with that clipper that doesn't make me look like a skinhead, not all the way down. They got different sizes, right?"

"Yeah, one is the lowest, that would be a little skin heady. Probably a four is what you're thinking." He held up his fingers to show Dwight the measurement. Dwight didn't really look.

"Four sounds good. Everything on top, and the beard too? Can you do the beard?"

"Yeah," he said hesitantly. "I'm just not sure about your bandage. I don't wanna mess with that."

"No, its cool, just go around it, if you don't mind, and just the clippers on the lowest setting. No, I uh, fell of a ladder at work and fell right onto this piece of metal, this uh thing, they had stuck up there, jabbed the shit outta me."

"Wow, hello workman's comp, huh? Dang."

"Yeah, I'll probably be a millionaire in a couple days."

"Ha ha, right on."

The guy was quick, but Dwight still suffered through it impatiently. All through the haircut, he thought about what to do with loose ends. When he brushed Dwight off and removed the cape, he looked in the mirror as he got up from the chair and saw a reduced version of himself. The bandage on his neck really stuck out now and he looked like he should be pulling around an I.V. stand. He thanked and paid him and left the old men to their busy day.

As he approached the truck, he looked in the window apprehensively to see how Dog was, and relaxed when he saw him with his head on his paws, sleeping. "You have a nice nap?" Dog raised his head slowly as Dwight got in the truck and wagged his nub a few times, then yawned. He reached over and patted his back softly. "You like my do? Look pretty sharp, huh?" Dog looked at him. "No? Pshh, what do you know, dumb dog."

He started the truck and sat there while it idled, staring down the street ahead. "What can I do with the money, Dog?" Dog had his head back down. Dwight looked over at him with concern. *He must really be hurting, the truck running and him with his head down.* He looked okay though. Just time, Dwight thought. But not with me. He looked down at him. *What am I gonna do with you?*

He didn't have much to give, and didn't have anyone to give it to. Maybe he should just leave it. Maybe some family member would sue him and they could have the money. He scoffed inside. *Yeah, so my uncle molested kids for twenty years and ruined dozens of lives, but you had no right to kill him. Now give me your money.*

"They'll probably get it, too," he mumbled. His mouth was dry and he suddenly wanted a drink. And right behind that thought was Belly and Karen. His spirits rose a little as he imagined giving them the money, but then dropped back down some as he imagined neither one would accept it. *Shit.* Well, he wanted a drink anyway, so maybe he would go by and feel Belly out a little. It was early afternoon and Karen wouldn't be there, but Belly would. He looked over at Dog. "Let's go have a drink, bud. Sliders later, yeah that's right, I said sliders." He had a thought and laughed. "You think White Castle would use it as an advertisement? Serial killer and his dog sidekick request fifty sliders as last meal!"

He drove through town seeing all of the businesses and houses out of the corners of his eyes. Today, maybe? Tomorrow? Would he ever drive down this street again? Whatever happened, he was glad he was going to The Shame. It was the only placed he cared for, the only place he felt comfortable. One more time.

He pulled into the empty parking lot and wondered how Belly made any money. The old Grenada held watch over the weeds and trash in the parking lot, and he saw Belly's truck sticking out around the corner of the building. He rolled the windows down about halfway. Dog peered out over the dash to see if they were at White Castle. He looked over at Dwight like *we lost?* He laughed inside.

"I said after. I'll be in here for a while, then we'll get stuffed man, I told you. I'd bring you inside, don't think he'd mind, but you're all gimped up. Just fucking lay back down, okay?" Dog looked at him sideways. "Look, I'll probably end up having to shoot you anyway, so shut the fuck up." He shut the door and went inside.

Belly was seated on a stool behind the bar. He had his reading glasses on and was looking at the paper intently. He looked up over his glasses as Dwight entered.

"Take those things off, old man, everybody knows you can't read. Prolly been sitting for three hours, waiting for somebody to come in and think you read the paper."

Belly put the paper and his glasses down on the bar and said, "Should I call the cops now before all the excitement begins, you know, just have 'em on stand by? Or can we wait awhile?"

Dwight relaxed a little at Belly's tone. He wasn't mad, or not too mad anyway. He didn't realize he was nervous until Belly started talking. The last time he'd been in here there'd been fighting, stuff had been broken, Karen had gone to the floor, and he had nearly been shot.

"Well it's just you and me in here. I can take you pretty easy, so no, I imagine we'll be alright." He smiled.

"Shit." He got up and made two drinks, and set one before Dwight. "No work today? You do have a job?"

Dwight dank half his drink slowly, feeling the soda and alcohol swirl around in his mouth and into his system, cold and biting. "Ahh. Yeah, I do. Well, I did. Maybe not." He smiled and tapped the side of his drink, looking at Belly. He finished the rest of it off, suddenly thinking they didn't serve alcohol in prison. Belly looked at his untouched drink and slid it over to Dwight, then made himself another one. Dwight picked up the new glass and drank half of it, the surge of sugar and alcohol tingling through his chest.

"Goddamn, we celebrating? Or have you had a bad week?"

Dwight held up two fingers to indicate the second option. "I'll probably get a new job here pretty soon, making license plates or something." Might as well get right into it.

Belly raised an eyebrow slightly as he took a drink, then chuckled, deciding Dwight was joking.

Dwight started again, "I'll, uh…probably be going to prison soon," he said flatly. He held Belly's eyes.

Belly set down his drink, then picked it up again and finished it. "Well, I hate to hear that. I just bought two cases of the cheapest vodka they sell." He gave Dwight a straight face.

Dwight laughed out loud for a few seconds. "Aw man, did you back the wrong horse. Well I'll drink as much as I can while I sit here. But I ain't paying for any of it. I won't be back again, so when I get done, I'm just gonna run out. You can't catch me."

There was an awkward silence as the joke dried up. He realized Belly didn't know what they were doing.

"I killed some people." He looked at Belly and Belly looked at him. "They had it coming, and I'd do it again. I ain't asking you to be a part of it, or listen to all my bull shit, but you know I've had a rough time, and this is the only place I come to where I don't hate myself and everything that is my life. This *is* probably the last time I'll be in here, and I need to get something settled."

He paused to let Belly digest what he had said. Belly's face was blank, but his eyes were awake. He grabbed a towel like he might wipe something, then just held on to it.

"I don't have much, but I don't have anyone to give it to either. You're gonna say no, so just don't for a minute. I don't have a lot of time to talk you into this, and I know we're not super close or anything, but I count you as a friend. My only friend, really. There's Karen. I really like her, and if I wasn't so fucked up, I'd try...to be more, with her. I'm not crying, I'm just saying. This bar is a shithole." He watched as Belly's face turned at the insult and he hurried on. "It's a great bar Belly, I love this fucking place. This bar is what most of us need. Some place to be something else for a little while, or just sit and relax and watch other people fuck up for change. What I mean, is it's a little old, and dated. You let just any old idiot in here, and he gets drunk on cheap ass vodka and tears shit up. I would like to make a donation."

Belly's face showed immediate refusal and he started to say something. Dwight cut him off. "I told you to just not say no for just a fucking minute, okay?" He let the request hang there, let all that he had said settle in and weigh down the air.

"They're gonna come get me, I think, and I'm not coming back. I'm going to give you a little of what I've got and you're gonna take it, I hope, and put some new ugly brown carpet on the walls, and buy some pool sticks that don't look like letters, and put some goddamn cushions on these goddamn stools. And do whatever else with it. Spend it on this bar, because it's what's kept me going." He choked up on the last part, raising his voice emphatically, embarrassing himself. He looked down at the bar forcing himself not to cry, silent now. He was tired of crying.

Belly said simply, "Okay. I can take a donation. You've torn up enough shit. " He got another glass and made Dwight another drink, and refilled his own. Dwight looked up at him imploringly. Belly gave a slight nod.

"Okay, okay," Dwight said softly. He got his checkbook out of his back pocket and raised his hand toward Belly, making a writing motion. Belly frowned a little and fished around the bar until he found one, handing it to Dwight. Dwight laughed inside. For some reason, men hated to give each other pens.

Dwight wrote a check for three thousand and left the name blank. He wasn't actually sure if Belly was his real name. He wrote out another one for two thousand and put Karen's first name on it, then asked

Belly what her last name was. Belly looked a little surprised but told him. Dwight wrote it down on the check. He handed Karen's to Belly.

"Would you give this to her please? She'll say no. Make her take it." He looked him in the eye. "Okay?"

"This one is for you and this bar. It's not a whole lot I know, sorry. If you can help your daughter out with some of it, please do. I'm not telling you what to do, but please don't, if she's just going to give it to her fuck up boyfriend." He handed him the check. Belly looked at them both and then back at Dwight.

"I'll hold on to these for a while," he said at last, unsure.

"No, don't. Go ahead and cash them at my bank. You can hold on to the cash for a while. I don't know what happens to your money and shit when you go to prison. Goes to your next of kin maybe, or just sits there, I don't know. I won't be coming back out, Belly. And I don't want any of it going to my dad and brother. My ex-wife, I'd like to give it to her, but I've messed with her life enough, and she wouldn't take it, anyway."

He sat back as Belly folded the two checks and put them in his shirt pocket. The vodka was mulling around gently in his head. He wanted another, but Belly seemed lost in space. "Get me a drink old man."

Belly gave him a strained smile and compiled, and then went in the back without saying anything. Dwight knew he was bothered but he didn't know what to do about it. He didn't think this would be fun. Belly came back in a minute later. Dwight watched his face and saw doubt.

"The money's not bad or tied to anything. The only thing I buy besides food and bills and stuff, is drinks in this place. I didn't have a great job, but the money's legit. They might come by and talk with y'all, maybe, I don't know. You can tell them the money was for damages. People can back you up on that." He smiled at Belly, and he smiled back, but not with his face.

He stared at Dwight. "What…the hell man? You killed someone? Who…why?"
Dwight hesitated, wanting to do this the short way.

"The thing that happened to my daughter…? I found some guys doing that to other kids, and I killed them for it. So that's it. I left some stuff at one guy's place and I think they'll find me soon." He paused. "I won't deny it."

Belly stood one hand leaning on the bar, shaking his head back and forth, working himself up to say something, then stopping. Then finally he said, "Those people, in the paper and news and stuff…? Was that you?"

Dwight looked at him evenly and held his eyes for a moment.

"Well, goddamn…" He pulled his hand off the bar and stood back, then put his hand back and leaned on the bar again. "No wonder you went all ape shit the other day. They're gonna get you, huh? What will they do?"

"I don't know." He finished off another drink. "I don't really give a shit. I have nothing…I want nothing…I'm done. Death penalty might be nice."

Belly stepped back and cleared his throat a little, the towel in one hand again. He didn't know what to do or what to say. It was making Dwight sad and uncomfortable. He didn't want this anymore. He had done what he wanted to do.

"Did you retire or something since I got here?" He looked plaintively at the two glasses with melting ice in them, and smiled around his face a little.

Belly's face scrunched up and he shook his head. "Oh shit, I'm just gonna make your goddamn drink in a beer pitcher from now on. Shit. Put a giant fucking straw in it." He snatched both of the glasses off the bar and filled them with ice and vodka and coke. "Well, I would if you was coming back."

Dwight lit a cigarette and they sat in silence for a bit. Belly went into the back and came out with a flat of glasses and started putting them at the different stations behind the bar.

Dwight said, "You need a dog? I got a good one for sale."

Belly had his back to Dwight and he answered without turning around. "Naw, I got a cat. Don't really care for dogs."

Dwight's heart sank a little. "A cat? And you don't like dogs? I don't think we can be friends anymore."

"My dad had dogs, mean ones. One of them attacked me one time, when I was little. My fault though, of course, you know, for getting too close to where he ate."

"He get rid of the dog?"

"No."

Dwight heard the conversation on that subject was now closed, and he said no more. Belly finished with the glasses and took the tray into the back. Dwight sat in silence, feeling the alcohol swim around in his head, smoking his cigarette.

A few minutes later, the front door to the bar banged open and sunlight crashed into the room and Dwight jumped on his stool.

"Oh my god, what happened to your DOG?"

Karen. The way she said the last word "dog" sounded like a gong being struck, two syllables. Dwight jumped off the stool suddenly worried, and said, "Why? Is he alright?"

"No, he's all beat up! Damn!"

"Is he still in the truck?" Dwight said quickly.

"Yeah, he's in there," she said mildly, having no idea the panic she had just caused in Dwight. "He's a good dog. He likes me."

"Oh shit, okay." Dwight sat back down, heart slowing, worried about Dog, then wondering what she was doing here.

She went around behind the bar and started making a drink. "You want a drink?" She finished it and set it down in front of him, next to his other full one, before he could answer. "Where's Belly? Belly! You ain't got no napkins out here! Oh no, wait, I found some!"

Belly came on from the back and said, "Hey kid." Karen hugged him and said, "Hey old man. Have you seen Dwight's dog, shit, he's all tore up! Dwight what happened to your dog?" She turned on him. "You fighin' him?"

"Huh, no, shit no. Goddamn, calm down. Here me and Belly was sittin' calm and gentle like, having a drink and talking loud enough so we could hear each other without the glasses breaking, and you blow in like a napalm bomb, yelling and disturbing two old guys just trying to relax. Goddamn Karen, you have your own special brand of loudness."

He looked her over and almost didn't try to hide the fact he liked her. He felt a little pinch in his chest. She was wearing a ball cap with her sandy blonde ponytail bouncing out the back and wearing a t-shirt, untucked, and some ugly plaid shorts. *Shit, my last day to see her and no cut-off blue jean shorts hugging her butt.*

"Two old coots sitting around farting, most likely," she said laughing.

"You got them cut-off blue jean shorts in the car?"

"Ha! No, why? You can't see my butt in these?" She turned and looked back at her butt.

"No. Can you run home and put them on and come back? I'll wait."

She laughed. "I can. You want me to? No, haha I'm not doing that."

Belly loomed ominously in front of Dwight and said, "I called her. You're gonna have to tell her that shit yourself." Then he walked off.

Well, thanks old man.

"Yeah, tell me what?" she walked up and stood in front of Dwight.

"Uh…" Dwight stammered.

"Is that your dog? What happened to him?"

He relaxed. *Okay, yeah, we can start there.*

"He, we, got into a fight. Him with two dogs, and me with this other dude. We won," he said a proudly. Then he said seriously, "I ended up killing that guy."

He let that sit there, and watched her face. It suddenly went serious.

"You *killed* him?" she whispered.

"Yeah, I went in there to kill him. He needed to be dead. I killed him and 3 others. They all needed to be dead. I don't need y'all to believe in me or back me up, I did it, I would do it again. These guys were doing some bad shit, I found out about it, and I killed them. The only reason I'm telling y'all, is I expect to go to jail soon, and I won't be coming back out." He paused, out of breath. He waited for her to explode, or pick up the phone, or just walk out. She might do that, just get her shit and leave. She stood in front of him leaning on the bar with both hands stretched out on the edge of the bar, her elbows locked, looking at him with her eyes shining intently, a frown flickering around her mouth. She was silent, for a moment.

"Why are you telling me this? You know I'm an accessory now," she said, agitated and a little upset.

"Well, no, you're not. You can tell someone if you like, but I don't think you will. Just the ramblings of a drunk anyway. I mean, I don't really want to get caught, but I didn't really put too much thought in it. There's more to this than I'm telling, but it's really not necessary. It's over now. I think it is. There's not many people that's important to me or I care about. I just wanted to give whatever I have to those I do care about who can use it. If you don't want it, okay. I don't need it anymore." He stopped, exhausted with it all.

"What are you talking about?" Her voice was high and a little loud.

Dwight looked at Belly. Belly gave a little shrug and looked back.

"You just said 'get down here, Dwight's gotten something to tell you'?"

Belly's face was blank. He gave a slight head nod.

Dwight sighed angrily. He started to bark it out, 'I'm going to prison so just take the fucking money or don't fucking take it' but he saw something new in Karen he had never seen before, uncertainty. She was absently trying to clean stuff up around her on the bar, but there was nothing to clean. He saw her hand shake. He looked up at her.

"Hey. Hey, you may not know this, but you're important to me. I come into this bar, dull and miserable, and I watch you work and talk to people and be yourself, and I feel better. Your laugh," he looked at Belly who smiled a little, "that wonderful laugh. The way you talk to people, like they matter. I watch you constantly." He paused, hoping he wasn't being too stalkery. "Especially your butt."

She smiled and gave a small laugh. "I know you watch me, dumbass." She paused and collected herself. "You seemed so sad all the time, I tried to make you smile. You never did anything though. I liked that, and I didn't like that."

He forced himself to stay silent. Whatever came out immediately would be stupid. He turned his head away slightly as his throat tightened up. He cleared his throat as he thought about what to say.

"I had a really bad time last year, something I don't plan to get over. By killing these four pieces of shit, I was able to make up for some of it. If I run across another one out there in the parking lot, I'll kill him too. If there's one walking down my sidewalk when I get home, I'll kill him. I'm done being a part of the regular world. You were the only thing that might have brought me back, but no. I would have drowned you right along with me. I like you too much for that."

They all were silent for a little while. He needed to finish up and get Dog situated.

"You and Belly and that dog are what I've got. I'm gonna get locked up, and that's okay. I have a little money and only two people to give it to. You just stop right there! You're gonna say the same thing Belly wanted to say, but don't! I wrote two checks out, one for you and one for Belly and this bar…and it's given with what love…I have left…" He barely got the words out, choked up with saying love. Tears filled his eyes and his nose clogged with snot, he put his head down to hide it and held up one finger for them to wait, to hold still until he recovered. He was embarrassed, but Jesus, what did it matter now. He put his hand down and found napkins in Karen's warm hand. He wanted to grab her and jerk her over the bar. He wiped his face and cleared his nose. They waited quietly. Karen fixed another drink.

He decided to not let them settle the matter of the money. He would move on.

"Belly won't take my dog Karen. Would you like him?" He felt the answer would be yes with all the emotion and her petting him already.

A long pause. "I can't. They don't allow dogs in my apartment. Sorry," she said meekly. "What about your family? They won't take your dog?" He gave a little head shake, no. "What about the shelter, huh? No, you probably don't want him to go there. You murdered four people?"

"Yes," he said quietly. "For good reason. Some people need to be dead. I'm sorry you came down here, but I'm glad to see you. I didn't want to dump all this on you both. Maybe I should have just left it. I'm sorry."

He was so buzzed right now, it almost made up for the mood. He wished she was wearing the shorts. She looked lost, and it didn't look good on her. He had to fix that.

"Y'all have been a friend to someone who doesn't have any friends. You've made my life better. I'm not a bad person. If you knew about these people, you'd know."

He looked up at her and smiled an unhappy smile. He stood up and looked at Belly, who was staring at him, and nodded his head. "I gotta go." He walked quickly out of the bar, managing to say, "I love you both," as he hit the door.

He begged her silently not to follow, but he was flooded with warmth when he heard the door open behind him. He turned and saw her coming out. Dwight was afraid for a moment of what to do.

She opened her arms and came to him, and he embraced her roughly. His check was next to her neck, her ponytail just in front of his face. She was gripping him tightly and he realized she was crying. He squeezed her back and smelled her hair. He didn't say anything for a while, then he felt she might be uncomfortable holding him like this so he tried to pull back a little but she refused with a little grunt and held onto him. They swayed for a few moments as her emotions receded. He was able to hold her now for her. He smelled her wonderful hair again and felt her neck against his cheek. He breathed her in, inhaled her deeply. He kissed her on the cheek and finally pulled back.

Karen looked at him, face beet red and wet and smeared. Somehow, she had a napkin and was drying her face. He smiled at her and she laughed a tinkling laugh.

She said, "I will take your money, if you want me to have it. I will. What do you want me to do with it? I can board your dog until I find someone for him? What about your bills, do you have them all paid? Do you want me to make a donation…?"

"Shut up," he said softly. "Oh my god can't you shut up? Don't do any of that. Please, make me happy by doing something with it that makes you happy, or just put it in savings. It's not that much anyway, sorry. I drink a lot." He smiled. She smiled and relaxed. She started to talk about her job suddenly, and he listened and listened. After a few minutes she seemed to realize she was rambling, and she finally slowed down. They walked over to the truck, and he opened the door and she fawned over Dog, and he about pissed himself getting in better positions for her to pet him. She went over all the ways she could think of to find him a home, and promised to get back with him when she found someone. He just listened, trying to record this time with her. She didn't have his number, and he didn't give it to her.

Later, he sat in the truck with it running, his hand ruffling through Dog's hair. He stared through the truck windshield out into the nearly deserted parking lot of The Shame. She was back inside, with

Belly. He wanted to leave soon, before she came out again to go home, but he was stuck for the moment.

"What a day...huh, Dog? What a day. That went pretty good." He lingered his mind over their short time in the parking lot together, some of the stuff in the bar, but mostly, being that close to her, knowing that she cared for him. He was content. His heart was light, and his mind was good. He needed nothing now. The police would come, and he would go. But then his bright day clouded over, and he looked down at Dog. He had no one to take him.

"Someone will take you, huh?" He looked at him lying there on the seat, sort of sad like, leg and neck shaved, one ear half gone now. He looked like trouble. If they take you to the pound, Dwight thought, the only one who would take you is a bleeding heart, someone who needs stuff to fix. His heart got a little heavy with this most important loose end that he didn't know what to do about.

He felt the pressure of leaving, before she came back out, and he put it in gear and left The Shame. He went to White Castle and ordered a 20 pack, half with and half without onions. He refused to let Dog have any while they drove, and Dog's eyes told the sad story of abuse and mistreatment. He kept his head down on the seat in protest until they pulled into the drive. He got Dog down then grabbed the sliders and they went inside. He had feared police cars might be at his house, and he had decided to keep going, immediately handing out the sliders until they got caught if he saw any, but the street and house were vacant.

They settled in and got stuffed on sliders, and Dwight watched one of those Fistful of Dollars movies with Clint Eastwood. Dog stretched out on the floor and digested his meal in sleep, occasionally releasing a pffft. Dwight suffered through them and let him sleep. Later, he took a shower and came back in the living room. The sun was beginning to set and he realized he was in a Clint Eastwood marathon, and he watched another movie before he suddenly thought about his truck. It was a work truck, but it was in pretty good shape. He went to the little safe he had and rummaged around until he found the title. He looked it over, trying to figure what to do, then signed it over to Karen. He wrote a letter out about how it belonged to her and where she could be reached, and left the letter in an envelope addressed to her on the kitchen table. He was happy with himself and went back to Clint Eastwood.

He had the blinds open on the living room window so he could see them when they came, and he woke to the sound of car doors shutting, and police cars were the first thing he saw. Dwight got up quickly and put his pants on, and then opened the door as they approached. He saw someone go by the side of the house through the window as he opened the door. They were slightly surprised and made cautious movements, taking a step back or resting a hand to gun. He held up his hands as he looked at a guy in a suit flanked by two uniformed officers crowded on the little porch.

"It's okay, it's okay. Whatever y'all are here for it's okay."

Dog stepped up next to him to see what was going on. One of the uniformed said, "Dog!" and grabbed at his gun, backing up. The other guys were momentarily undecided until Dog started growling.

Dwight dropped to his knees by Dog and said, "Stop, stop! It's okay. No, no man," he said to the officer with his hand ready on his gun. "It's okay man! We're good, okay? Please?" He held up his right hand and held on to Dog with his left, talking quickly and reassuringly to him.

The man in the suit said, "Are you Dwight Harris?"

"Yes I am. If you're going to arrest me, y'all come inside. All I got in here is this dog, and he's cool if y'all are cool. If you come in on me as a group he won't like it. I don't want him to get shot. He's a good dog just come on in okay? Don't shoot him."

The man in the suit surveyed the situation for a moment and said, "Okay, we'll come inside, no problem." He said over his shoulder, "Shoot the dog if he gets stupid."

Dwight stayed kneeling with Dog as the man in the suit entered with one of the uniformed officers. The one with his hand on his gun waited for Dwight to enter, then followed behind. Dog looked them over as they came in and sniffed a knee as it went by. He looked over at Dwight. Dwight knew he was good. "You're a good dog."

The last officer watched this and then stepped easily into the house. He put his hand out palm up near Dog's nose. Dog sniffed it intently for a moment then walked around the other men, checking them out.

Dwight turned to the man in the suit.

The man in the suit said, "I'm Detective Rich Bishop. Dwight Harris, you are under the arrest for the murder of…" When he finished his speech he said, "Can we handcuff you now, or is this dog going to eat us?" The officer who entered last had knelt down and was scratching Dog's good ear, gently looking over his wounds.

"Yes, he's good."

He nodded at the other uniform, who got Dwight's hands behind his back and cuffed them. "Go let him in the back," he said to the other uniform, who went to the back door and let in another uniformed police officer. With a motion from the detective, the new uniform went and searched through the rest of the small house.

The officer who had petted Dog said, "He was there, with you. Wasn't he?" He turned his head and looked up as Dwight. They all looked at Dwight and waited.

"At the last one, yes."

There was an odd little silence. The officers exchanged glances. Detective Bishop said, "There are more?"

Dwight said, "Three others. Three separate ones. Four total."

He got something out of his jacket and said to Dwight, "Can I record this?" Dwight nodded, and then he told them the basic details about the three others.

They stood silent while he spoke. Dog made his way around their legs, checking the new officers who had come back into the room and going around again to everyone else. The one officer knelt down again and gave him some attention.

After Dwight finished, they suffered through a short silence, then the detective said, "I'm confused...*why* did you kill all these people?" He said it like Dwight might be mentally unstable, like they might be dealing with a psycho, and he didn't really want a real answer, he was just being a big detective, all important, in a suit. Cops in suits, Dwight thought. He let his anger rise.

"Cause they were fucking child molesters. You get me? You can arrest them, if you can catch them at it. I just kill them. You're welcome." He said the last rather mildly.

One of the cops snorted. The detective said, "How did you know they were child molesters? Did you watch them or something?"

Dwight didn't want to really explain how he knew and have it all over the local media that he was psychic or something, or worse, that he had received a gift from his dead daughter.

"I just know. I have a thing, I can tell. The daycare place? That guy, you know he was doing it. Get in touch with that church and interview the parents and kids, that choir director was doing it. I sent them a letter. You'll find something on him. The first guy, he was doing it when I walked in on him. I don't know what the girl said about him. I don't care because he won't be doing it anymore. She needs counseling. That last guy?" He waited and saw looks pass between them. "You saw his movies?" He waited again. Eyes glanced here and there, and he saw a slight nod from the detective. "Yeah. I'd kill him again."

Bishop said, "So just the four murders?" Dwight nodded his head yes. "Did you commit any other crimes you want to admit to now?"

Dwight ignored the question. "Just the four murders. I didn't kill the fifth one." He paused as they looked at him. "He's a cop. I wanted to kill him, but, well…he's a cop. So I didn't." They looked at him and then at each other, a flicker of understanding.

"You know Officer Lopez?" He wondered if anyone here was Lopez's buddy.

One of the uniformed officers spoke up sternly, "You ain't saying he's a child molester? You're not saying that, are ya?" His fire faded just a bit at the last. No one else backed him up.

"Only if you count raping your 15 year old step-daughter." Dwight took a step toward him, suddenly mad. "IS THAT A CHILD MOLESTOR? Yeah, he's fucking doing it, and he'd be dead right now if he wasn't a cop. I wrote the letters and he needs to be put down, or put in jail. I guess going to jail is a pretty bad thing for cops. He needs to get there pretty soon."

They all looked at each other, or down at the floor, and one shook his head and whispered to another.

"Well, that's a different thing. We got you and hopefully you're it. I'm tired of this shit," the detective said. "Let's go."

"What about my dog?" Dwight said, voice rising slightly.

Detective Bishop said, "You got somebody we can call, to come get him? We can put him in the backyard till then."

"No, I got nobody. I've been trying to give him away. I figured y'all were coming soon."

"Why'd you figure that?"

Dwight looked at him. "You found my prints on the knife, I guess?"

They all looked around at each other again. "No, not yet." He looked at Dwight, waiting.

Dwight looked at him back. "Did one of the neighbors call it in or something? I don't know, what the fuck?"

Detective Bishop twirled his finger in the air, indicating the upper corners of the walls. "He had cameras. Everywhere. We watched you, just walk on in there and try and get yourself killed. He couldn't get in the back door at first," he said, pointing at Dog. "Then he backed up and jumped through that screen door. Sailed in there like a bullet."

He looked down at Dog who was sitting by his leg. "We wouldn't be talking if I didn't have this dog," Dwight said softly. Dog looked up at him. *When are they leaving?*

"Never, buddy," he whispered down to him.

One of the officers said to the one who had been petting Dog, "What about you Mike?""

The other uniform who was not Mike shook his head and made a slight tsk noise at him to shut up. Dwight looked at the officer called Mike. His face went serious and he looked down at Dog slowly, still by Dwight's side. The other officers went silent and waited. He knelt down and made a small noise, and Dog limped easily over to him and sniffed the hand he held out. Mike petted his head as Dog sat down.

"His name is Dog, though he would probably answer to anything if you take him to White Castle."

There was a short laugh from one of the uniformed officers.

Mike petted Dog and then looked up at Dwight. "Like the John Wayne movie?" He smiled and Dwight felt a twinge in his chest. Dog could go with him.

"He's a good dog, man." Dwight waited.

Mike stood up finally and nodded his head. "I had a K-9 for awhile. I'll take him if he'll go with me."

The detective said, "You gonna take him back to the station, or what?"

"I was almost done when they called me for this. I can head home, if you don't need me."

The detective looked over at Dwight, "Do we need him?"

"No, man."

"Yeah, take him home. There's no need to say anything about this to anyone is there?" He put the question to the room, but he wasn't really asking. The room was quiet, a few head shakes of agreement.

Dwight knelt down awkwardly in the cuffs and said, "Dog." His one ear perked up and he looked in Dwight's direction and came immediately over. Dwight leaned his head into Dog's neck.

"You're a good damn dog, you know that?" he said softly. "I don't know why you felt like hanging out with me, but I'm glad you did. Glad you did, man."

He suddenly felt a hand on his arm and he thought he was being jerked up, but then the handcuffs slid off his wrists.

He pulled Dog close and hugged him. He whispered softly in his ear, "You're the best friend I ever had. You saved what was left of my life. There's little kids all over town thanking you right now, buddy. We did some good shit, Dog, I don't care what they say." Dog wasn't sure what was happening, but it sounded pretty good. He wasn't much of a licker, but he tried to get in several right now. Dwight let him do his thing, knowing he would never get another chance to feel this dog's tongue on his face. Then he said, "Okay, okay. Back up, dummy. You're gonna go with this guy here. He's one of the good ones. You can work with him now. Maybe he'll let you ride in front and hit the siren. I don't know about the sliders, though. He looks pretty healthy, like he might try and take care of you. Feed you dog food with vegetables and shit in it. Well, there's nothing I can do about that now man."

He wiped his eyes on his shirt and stood up. The officers adjusted themselves, and Mike looked at them both with sad smile.

The officer with the cuffs stepped over and Dwight turned his back and gave him his hands and he put the cuffs back on. They escorted him out of the house and walked him to a police car. People driving down the street were slowing, and his old neighbor was standing in the lawn with his wife, hose in hand, watching with interest. Dwight watched Mike lead Dog over to his police car. He opened up the driver's side door and told him to get in, which Dog did with a little limping hop. The last he saw of him was through the glare of the windshield, sitting up in the front seat, looking straight ahead.

CHAPTER 12

The days that followed were interesting, and boring. He sat in the cell alone, a lot. Then there would be flurries of lawyers and investigators asking this and that, and head shakings. They all wondered how he knew. He never said, and he wasn't going to.

His court appointed lawyer was a little stupid. He tried hard at first to mount a defense, but seemed confused by Dwight's easy admittance to the crimes. Dwight finally settled his mind and told him he wasn't going to lose this case. It was already lost, so to speak.

"I killed 'em, dude. Let's move on."

Dwight kind of enjoyed his lawyer's visits after that. He relaxed, and they talked about his other cases and his girlfriend, and his mom. Dwight's plateau for enjoyment was pretty low.

When the media got the story in its sights things began to liven up. It was like a boulder pushed over a hill, slow and lumbering until it bounced off enough rocks to really get going, then it vaulted high in the sky and smashed heavy into the ground. Dwight watched it all unconcerned. He answered questions bluntly and only avoided how he actually knew. They couldn't be happier. 'The Child Molester Killer', they tried to call him. CMK. He thought the reporters must have had a race to find a nickname. They probably sat up at night thinking catchy names, trying to be the first one. It was stupid he thought, and didn't stick, not really. They were all excited to have some fresh exciting news to sell more commercials with, but he was a boring serial killer, in personality anyway. He gave them nothing, said nothing. The idea that he might have some way to tell if a person was molesting children was fascinating and they tried to make as much of that as they could. He didn't pay it any attention though.

Karen and Belly came to see him once, before the end of the trial. It was unexpected, and his heart rose to the top of his chest then plummeted to his feet within a moment. He didn't want to see them.

He resigned to see them, fearing a little that Karen would get her feelings hurt if he didn't. He was immediately disappointed when he saw her through the glass, wearing makeup and looking nervous. *Goddamn.* Her hair was all curly like she had it permed and hanging down on her shoulders stiffly. And she was wearing glasses, big round ones. Belly was seated behind her and he looked past her and caught Belly's eye.

What the fuck man?

It was her idea. She cares about you so shut the fuck up.

He sat down and smiled at her warmly. She had the phone in her hand and was already speaking into it rapidly. He picked the receiver up and put it to his ear patiently.

"…find my stupid fucking contacts. And so, how are you? Are you eating? Is the food good? Can I bring you something? I know, my hair looks stupid. Belly, ask them if I can bring in those muffins. Did you ask?"

She kept talking and Dwight warmed over inside watching the two of them. Belly looked confused and unsure, but slowly stood up, looking around for a guard to ask about the muffins. Dwight caught his eye quickly and shook his head no slightly, smiling with his eyes. Belly looked relieved and shrugged and sat back down.

"…you sure you want me to have your truck? I mean, it's not a bad truck, thank you. I'd drive it. I like it. You don't have any family you want me to give it to? I'll sign the title right over to them, drive it to wherever they are, I don't mind. I'll get a cab back. Huh? You eating?"

He looked at her and willed her to stop. He smiled again and said, "You're hair looks great." She started to smile then constricted her face and put her head in her hand for a brief moment. He realized how nervous she was. "I eat better in here than I did at home. They don't' have White Castle…so."

She smiled this time and relaxed. And then there she was, collected and ready.

"How's your lawyer? Does he know what he's doing? I worked for a lawyer in Jessup County, and she was damn good. I'll call her right up."

He held up his hand to slow her. "He's good, he's good. He's kind of hamstrung though, you know, by the fact that I did it. I'm good ,Karen. I'm

where I'm supposed to be. I don't have any worries."
He looked at her and watched it settle in, that she
couldn't help. "You and my dog are the only things
I'll miss." He smiled and waited for Belly to get
offended. He gave Dwight a sour look, and Dwight
laughed at him.

"Tell him I can't drink in here, so he ain't
really worth much to me anymore."

"What? I will not! Belly, he says he can't drink
in here so you ain't worth much. He's stupid. Oh my
god."

She talked about a few more things; the food,
the inmates, his lawyer again, the bar. And then there
was nothing left to talk about and he watched her
sadly as she ran out of things to say.

"Will you write to me?" he asked suddenly. "I
mean, just every now and then, nothing important.
Just, you know, getting mail will probably be nice in
here."

"Yeah! Oh yeah, I'll write, okay." He could tell
it made her nervous for some reason. He suddenly
felt glad and a little bit alive that he had someone he
cared about.

"You can give them your address, I think, and
they'll give it to me. I'll write first, and then,
whenever, you can tell me how the bar is and if Belly
is getting fatter.

She laughed a little, but not with her eyes. He
thought now she might have cried before they got
here, and imagined she might cry again later today.

He felt bad that she was attached to him like this.
But he would write to her, and he guessed she would
write back a few times, and then he would let her go.
But he'd have her letters.

Belly got on the phone for a few minutes and Dwight told him thanks, and to look out for Karen. Belly told him to take care of himself in there and they both realized he might not have much control over that. But it was what it was.

He was found guilty of three of the murders. They left one in reserve to try him on later in case something happened. He got three life sentences and the amount of time he was meant to serve in prison rested on his shoulders like a truckload of wet cement being slowly poured on them. He played it all off like he didn't give a shit, and he thought he didn't. But he began to worry about one thing. He thought he might go crazy spending the rest of his life in close confines with the child molesters in prison. He was worried about that. He was 46 years old and if he didn't get killed in here, he could expect to spend 30-40 years in prison, until he died. It numbed his mind to think of nothing but concrete walls and bars and wire and the same routine and the same food and the same angry men everywhere, and that smell, day after day, for the next thirty years. He soon decided suicide would present itself in there somewhere and he would not last ten years. That made him feel better.

He was finally transferred to his new and last home a month later. They drove him seven hours in a van, just him and two guards. The van stank slightly of the smell. Not from the guards; the van itself. They chatted a lot and tried to get him involved. He finally realized they seem to have a certain amount of respect for him. He didn't know what to make of that.

They delivered him on time and handed him over all cuffed and chained. Papers were signed and people were talked to, and he was ushered here and there. Some were obviously excited to see him and knew something about him, and some were indifferent, dulled by the intense negative nature of their work.

He was finally handed over to two big guards, who were going to take him to his cell. One was a big older, black man and the other was a pudgy but serious looking, white man of about fifty. He guessed the black man was over sixty. They were polite to him but nothing else. He went were they said without question, so they had no problem.

He couldn't help but be a little amused at how movie-like it was starting to become. Once the boring paperwork and checking in was done and he approached the gate to what he guessed was his cell block, it was just like a movie, with the two big guards, one black and one white, and him shuffling along, chained at the hands and feet. He imagined people would be hanging their arms out of their cells through the bars, rattling tin cups and making cat calls at him, spitting on him and saying things like "fresh meat". He almost smiled, but he kept catching the linger of the smell. It was everywhere, strong here, faint there.

They stopped at the gate and started the procedures to open it. He looked into the long block; just like the movies, three stories high with cells on both sides and stairs winding up to the next levels. It was quiet though. It was about 3 pm, and he wondered if they were all out in the yard or something. The procedures were met, and the gate rattled open, and they motioned for him to go through. He shuffled past the gate with both guards at his sides, and he saw men standing at the bars of their cells watching, or getting up from their bunks to come see. He heard a shout, kind of a whoop, and then a loud call from the first cell he had past.

"Heyyyyyy!" Like an alarm. And then the place woke up. It was a low rumble of voices, calling and speaking, getting louder and louder. He glanced sideways at the guards, but they just kept walking. The clamor began to rise as they started yelling and banging and jumping. He thought they seriously can't get this wound up every time a new inmate arrives. He saw the black guard look over at the white guard with his eyebrows raising, and the white guard looked back and smiled and shrugged, and the black guard gave a big grin and turned his face forward and said, "I told you." They were shouting at him or to each other or at the guards, he wasn't sure, and then he saw and heard many of them clapping and whooping, and soon it was a deafening racket of clapping and cheering. Most of them were smiling at him. They kept walking down the long block, and he hoped they just kept on walking and never stopped.

They got to the end of the cell block and they led him up the stairs to the third floor. Occasionally he made eye contact with an inmate. Some smiling, some yelling, and many chanting "CMK!"

Everywhere was the smell. His head began to ache from the noise and the smell. He would die in here from that smell.

They neared the end of the block on the third floor, and he felt the white guard pull on his left arm and the black guard came around on his right, and they stopped in front of a cell. The noise was dying down from the lower floors ,and the inmates were beginning to settle some down there but it was still a clamor on the third floor. He peered into the cell as they called on their mic to open the door. One of them spoke into the cell and someone inside answered with the appropriate response, and the cell door slid open almost without a sound.

Dwight saw a tall white male standing at the back of the cell, his hand on the bunk. He was pudgy and bald. He was about Dwight's age, maybe younger, and pale with a sheen of sweat on his upper lip. The smell was in the cell, like someone had farted ten minutes ago, and Dwight was momentarily confused, and he realized the smell was muted everywhere he had been; the city jail, the van and here. He thought maybe it was because these men had been locked up and unable to do what it was they did. He studied the man in the cell, searching. He was smiling.

They started to move him into the cell and he stopped. They tensed and looked at him.

"What is he in for?" Dwight asked them.

"Never you mind what he in here for. He's happy to see you, and he won't cause you no problem. He ain't done nothing like what I hear you don't like. Ain't that right Max?"

Max opened a mouth with with stained and missing teeth and said, "Just car jacking! Ha ha!" He shifted his weight from foot to foot, looking nervously at Dwight.

They showed Dwight a little respect by waiting for him a moment to go into the cell on his own.

The other guard said, "It takes some getting used to. You'll be alright man."

Dwight inhaled the stench all around, almost seeing it come off of his cellmate like heat waves. He was still smiling at Dwight like he might smile at a Cobra.

It doesn't matter. I'll be in solitary confinement soon anyway. He stepped into the cell.

Cliff Roberts

ABOUT THE AUTHOR

Cliff Roberts is 46 years old and lives with his wife, Karla, and their two kids in the small town of Farmington in the southeast of Missouri, though they are all from the great state of Texas. Seriously, it's just too hot there. He graduated from Texas State University in 1994 with a degree in psychology and writing. His kids play soccer year round in St. Louis, and he and his wife occasionally play on the weekends with other old people. He has written stories sporadically since he was 16 but never got serious about writing a book until a few years ago when he wrote the first half of this book, and then he stopped. It just wasn't there anymore. Recently, he spent some months back in Texas working, and during the boring hours alone in the hotel room, he picked up the story, and to his delight, found it was there again. He has 12 more books in mind and is working furiously on them whenever his family does not bother him.

The Avenger in the Rye

Made in the USA
Thornton, CO
06/28/23 17:21:27

67527749-dcd3-46ab-a3e6-a74343241e0dR01